BARRACUDA

ALSO BY IRVING A. GREENFIELD

The Ancient of Days
Aton
High Terror

BARRACUDA

by Irving A. Greenfield

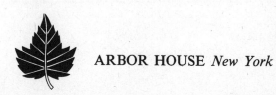 ARBOR HOUSE *New York*

WITH MUCH THANKS TO
CAPTAIN CLARK M. GAMMELL, UNITED
STATES NAVY

BARRACUDA

I

Monday, November 13
1950 hours

Low in the east, the moon was a burnished silver, and on the bridge of the *African Wolf,* the last dog watch was almost over. The *Wolf* was a C-2 type cargo ship, built in Mobile, Alabama, toward the end of World War II. Her best speed, even in a calm sea, was ten knots. Her sides were scabrous with rust and the cabin amidships a rust-streaked, dingy gray. In anything more than a moderate sea, she sailed badly, sometimes just barely holding steerageway.

Silently, Bernardo Themir, the ship's first officer, smoked his pipe and looked out to the horizon, where the star-studded sky rested on an ebony sea. A short man with a barrel chest, hairy, muscular arms and a weather-beaten face, he had been aboard ship for the last five years. Sooner or later he figured to become its captain but for that he'd have to wait until the old man retired, or died. Themir wasn't in a hurry, though; he didn't mind waiting for one or the other to happen.

Themir glanced at the helmsman. The man was new, a Greek, at least that's what his papers said. It made no difference on the *Wolf,* no two men were from the same country here. Most of them were derelicts anyway, who would jump ship as soon as they had enough money for a long drunk. Few ever signed on the *Wolf* for more than one trip.

With a shrug, Themir walked out to the portside wing and knocked his pipe against the railing, watching the dead ashes drift into the sea, then, unscrewing the stem, blew through it to clear away any trapped saliva. To the west several large clouds lowered on the horizon and flashes of heat lightning intermittently turned the night sky white. He hoped a squall wasn't bearing down on the *Wolf,* or worse, the beginnings of a real storm. The *Wolf* still had a good three days' sailing before it reached San Juan, and he hated the thought of spending it in rough seas, especially since the ship was riding low in the water with a full cargo.

He was just about to step back into the wheelhouse to make a radar scan when the first explosion tore the ship apart, killing him instantly. Secondary explosions followed in rapid succession; the sea pouring into the engine room, rupturing high-pressure steam pipes, spewing live steam into the faces of the screaming men.

Four minutes after the first explosion, the *African Wolf* lay dead in the water and began to list sharply to portside.

The first explosion had thrown the radio officer from his chair. Wincing now with pain, he lifted himself off the sloping deck and switched his transmitter to 2182 Megahertz, the emergency frequency. *"May Day . . . May Day . . . This is the African Wolf. . . the African Wolf. . . Position as of noon fifteen degrees north latitude . . . All ships in the vicinity . . . All ships in the vicinity . . . May Day . . . May Day . . . Noon position fifteen degrees north latitude, fifty-five west longitude . . . May—"*

Another blast hurled the radio officer against a metal cabinet, smashing the right side of his skull.

The *African Wolf* turned over on her portside and broke apart. The bow section sank first.

Of the thirty-eight crewmen aboard the ship, three landed in the water alive. One of them was the Greek helmsman. But none of them knew how to swim. They drowned, calling to each other for help and then to God. . . .

When dawn came, the three large patches of oil slick stained the blue water an ugly brown, and some debris bobbed up and down. Floating nearby were a dozen yellow life jackets with the ship's name clearly visible . . . but the patches of oil slick, the debris and the life jackets had already drifted several kilometers to the northeast of where the *African Wolf* had gone down.

II

Thursday, November 16th
0530

Lieutenant James Healy gazed out from behind the controls of the modified RF4 Phantom all-weather fighter, and grinned. His aeronautical engineering degree had got him assigned to an air-to-air missile evaluation team, but you had to put in airtime, too, to keep your flying status. But Healy didn't mind; he liked flying. Especially this baby: with her increased reconnaissance capabilities she'd do just about anything for you.

Healy was twenty-five years old, lean, medium height, his boyish face marked with freckles beneath his blond hair. Matter of fact, he thought, he enjoyed flying more than anything except a good roll in the sack, and, hell, maybe even more than that, because of the sense of freedom it gave him. No matter what they claimed, women were always trying to lock a man up, tie him into some sort of a commitment. Sometimes they didn't even know they were doing it, but most of the time they went at him with everything they had, from what they did in bed to the way they cooked dinner for two . . . Healy didn't want any sort of involvement; he was having too damn much fun just the way things were.

He settled back. Healy was on a predawn flight out of the naval air station at Roosevelt Roads, Puerto Rico, and had been in the air about forty-five minutes now. By the time the clouds in the east were about to turn pink with the sun, he realized he was flying close to where the *African Wolf* had gone down. Before taking off, he had been told by the operations officer about the ship's May Day call. . . .

"Since you'll be over that way," Lieutenant Commander Riggs had said in his southern drawl, "might as well go down and have a look-see. Not that I think you'll find anything . . . Been days since she sank and nothin's been spotted." He snapped his fingers. "Gone just like that. Ship and men . . . I'm glad the press wasn't too interested, or we'd have another Bermuda Triangle to explain."

"Any guess as to what happened?"

"Nope . . . but things like that happen at sea . . . She was an old ship and her boilers just might have had it. She was carrying sixty drums of chemicals with her bulk dry cargo, you know, wouldn't have taken much to set her off. One of the few remaining tramps around . . . Well, we'll probably never know."

"I'll look around," Healy answered, getting up to leave the ready room.

"You want to try an air refueling?" Riggs asked.

"Might as well . . . I'm goin' to have to do it sometime. Now's as good as later."

"We'll tell you where to rendezvous with the tanker."

Healy nodded and left the room. A short time later, he had been at the controls of the RF4, roaring down the runway to gain airspeed. . . .

The plane was on automatic pilot now, Healy holding her altitude at one thousand meters. From time to time, he spoke to CPO Dominic Monte, a radioman at Roosevelt Roads, feeding him his latitude and longitude as they showed up on the position indicator unit of the aircraft's rumb-line computer. Healy knew Monte from months of speaking to him over the radio and they'd long ago become friends, drinking together in San Juan, finding women . . .

"I have an update on the weather," Monte said.

"Let me have it."

"Thundershowers moving in from the sou'west, traveling at fifteen knots."

"How does that affect my refueling?"

"No word on that yet."

Their conversation was terse and concerned only with the mission. Neither man would think of tying up the channel with personal chit-chat. When Monte was out of contact with Healy, he was communicating with some other pilot. If there was some discernible difference in the way they spoke to each other, perhaps it was in their tone; now and then it was subtly less staccato, a sly hint of a previous night's carousal sneaking in.

Healy read out his latitude and longitude, noting that his position corresponded with the last known position of the *African Wolf.* He saw nothing, but to make sure, dropped down to one hundred and fifty meters, flew in a wide circle and then climbed back up again.

"Report negative on debris or survivors," Healy said.

"I read you."

"Any word about my refueling?" Healy would have preferred not to do it in a thundershower. To come in at the right angle so that the boom from the tanker made contact on the first pass was tricky enough in good weather, but in a thundershower there was a real problem with turbulence. Healy realized that if it was a tactical situation, he'd have to refuel no matter what the condition of the weather was, but right now—

"Negative on refueling," Monte answered.

"Changing course . . . new heading 014 degrees . . . I repeat, changing course . . . new heading 014 degrees . . . stand by." Healy took over the controls of the aircraft. "On new heading . . . fourteen degrees . . . Will maintain course for fifteen minutes and then change to—" Abruptly Healy saw what looked like an oil slick off his portside.

"Flight two . . . flight two . . . do you read me?" Monte said.

"Five by five," Healy repeated. "Sighted what appears to be oil slick off my port side . . . going down for a closer look."

"Standing by."

Healy switched on the aircraft's photographic equipment

and, banking sharply to the left, pointed the nose of the ship straight at the oil slick.

"Coming up on it."

Monte didn't answer.

"Positive," Healy said, passing over at seventy-five meters. "Positive ID of oil slick." At the lower altitude the slick looked darker than at a thousand meters, and he saw it was dotted with debris. He made three more sweeps over the area, clicking off more photographs.

"This is Riggs," the operations officer said.

"Yes, sir."

"Did you see any signs of survivors?"

"Negative . . . visual sighting of life jackets."

"Return to base," Riggs said. "Return to base. Refueling exercise canceled."

"Read you," Healy answered. Monte must have notified Riggs the moment he had reported the oil slick; Riggs had spoken to him through a radio hook-up with his phone.

"Flight two," Monte called. "Flight two visibility at base three miles and diminishing rapidly . . . wind one hundred and ten degrees at fifteen knots gusting to twenty-three . . . will advise at five-minute intervals."

"Read you." Healy made one last pass over the oil slick before going back, this time coming in at one hundred meters from northwest. Three seconds past the area, he started to ease back on the stick and the ship's needle nose began to lift . . . and that's when he saw it: on a long, sloping diagonal out in front of him, the low dark silhouette of a submarine.

Immediately, he pushed the stick forward. A submarine submerged or on the surface was instantly considered an enemy unless otherwise identified. Even as Healy headed for the submarine, he radioed, "Visual contact with a sub."

"Say again?" Monte said.

"Visual contact with a *sub* . . . latitude fifteen degrees, twenty-six minutes; longitude fifty-five degrees forty-three minutes." He repeated the coordinates again and asked to have the rest of the conversation taped.

"Tape has been switched on from initial report of sub," Monte told him.

"Poseidon-type craft," Healy said, trying to keep the excitement out of his voice. "Visual contact . . . Sub appears to be Poseidon type."

He pushed the throttle forward and came roaring toward it. Jesus. *"Men on bridge* waving and pointing up at me," he reported, sweeping over the submarine at fifty meters. Quickly, he clicked off pictures, then pushed the jet into a steep climb, made a tight turn and roared down at the submarine again, this time wiggling his wings.

He switched his radio to another frequency and tried to make contact with the submarine, but nothing—"She's going down," Healy radioed his base. "She's diving!"

He pulled up, made another tight turn and went back over the submarine. He could just about make out her shape beneath the sea but within moments it had gone too deep.

"Flight two," Monte called. "Operations is on."

"Lieutenant, did you try to make radio contact?" Riggs said.

"Yes, but they did not respond."

"Are you sure about your visual ID?"

"Yes, sir."

"As soon as you land, report to the base commander's office."

"Yes, sir."

"Did you photograph it?"

"I have sixty shots on my first overflight and"—he checked the counters for the wing cameras—"another hundred on the wings."

"Very good, Lieutenant, very good indeed . . . return to base."

"Yes, sir." Healy waited a moment for the operations officer to get off the channel, then asked for another weather check.

"Rain," Monte said. "Wind at twenty knots from one hundred and fifteen degrees, gusting to thirty."

"Returning to base," Healy said.

"I read you."

Healy took a deep breath, then slowly let it out again. He realized he was wet with sweat. Pulling back on the stick and putting on his oxygen, he brought the ship up to thirty-five thousand feet and headed for home base . . . If that submarine was one of ours, he pitied its captain. The poor bastard would have a lot of explaining to do about being caught on the surface that way. . . .

But then if it wasn't one of ours . . . Prickles raced down his back and he began to sweat again. . . .

III

Thursday, November 16th
0730

Sheets of water sprayed up as the wheels of Healy's jet touched down and he raced along the rain-soaked runway. Quickly reversing thrust, he slowed the plane enough to turn off the runway, and carefully steered the RF4 into the parking area. A member of the ground crew guided him to a place on the apron and signaled him to cut the ship's engines, then several more crewmen swarmed over the ship, opening its canopy and helping Healy out of the cockpit.

Even before he touched the ground, two jeeps came racing up to the plane. He really was getting the royal treatment today, Healy thought.

One of the jeeps disgorged a Marine sergeant, who walked up to Healy and said in a midwest twang, "Will you please come with me, sir? Admiral Tunner is anxious to meet with you."

Healy nodded and gestured to the Marines in the other jeep. "Why are they here?"

"To guard your plane, sir. Intelligence has placed it off limits to all personnel without written permission from the base intelligence officer."

Healy pursed his lips but kept silent. How much did the sergeant know? Probably nothing.

"Looks like the rain's passing over," the sergeant commented cheerfully as the two of them climbed into the jeep. Healy agreed but made no attempt to continue the conversation. So he was going to see Tunner himself . . . Healy had met the Admiral the first day he'd been on base and seen him now and then in the Officers' Club, after that, but they'd never so much as exchanged nods. By all accounts, the man was a real terror, old navy, the kind who didn't care much for the changes that had been taking place recently.

"Are you assigned to the Admiral?" Healy asked.

"Yes, sir, I've been with him as long as he's been here . . . Going on three years next month."

Healy lapsed back into silence and sat with his own thoughts until, about fifteen minutes later, they pulled up in front of the base headquarters building. The sun was out by now, the sky overhead a lovely blue, the dark clouds well to the west, moving out over the mountains. . . .

The sergeant escorted Healy directly into the anteroom of the Admiral's office and told the attractive Wave at the desk, "The Admiral is expecting Lieutenant Healy." With a slight nod, she tilted her head to one side and picked up the phone. "Lieutenant Healy is here, sir," she said into it, scanning the young officer with a frankly curious gaze. Another slight nod. "You can go right in." The smile she gave him was not totally brisk.

"Thank you," said Healy, and knocked softly on the door.

"Come!" A deep voice called out.

Healy turned the shining brass knob and stepped inside. The Admiral was not at his desk. His heart hammering, Healy stopped and looked around the room. He took in its size, the American flag in one corner, the Admiral's two-star flag in the opposite corner, the highly polished mahogany desk. Then he saw Tunner himself, his back to him, standing in front of a large window that looked out over a green lawn, some bushes with bright red flowers and the curving trunk of a palm tree.

The Admiral wore his whites. As he turned, Healy had to remind himself that he was in his fifties. Tall, trim and still very muscular, Tunner could have been taken for a younger man, even though his black hair was flecked with gray. He had a strong chin, somewhat narrow lips and grayish green eyes.

For the few moments, neither of them spoke a word, then suddenly Healy remembered where he was and quickly said, "Lieutenant Healy, reporting as ordered, sir."

Admiral Tunner gazed at him for a minute more, then, slowly, "You've had a remarkable morning, Lieutenant

. . . Yes, I would say you've had quite a remarkable morning."

Healy remained silent. Was he being rebuked for something? He couldn't tell from the Admiral's tone whether he'd done anything wrong . . . he quickly checked his memory of the events that just happened . . . no, everything seemed by the book.

The Admiral was behind his desk now, and motioning Healy toward the chair at the left side. "The base intelligence officer will be here shortly," he continued. "But in the meantime, why don't you tell me what happened just prior to your alleged sighting of a submarine."

Healy sat down and in a soft voice replied, "Begging the Admiral's pardon, but the photographs will eliminate any doubt that what I saw was a sub."

"In our conversation, the object you saw will be referred to as an *alleged* submarine."

"Yes, sir."

"Please tell me exactly what happened."

Healy repeated everything just as he remembered it, from the moment he'd sighted the oil slick and debris to the disappearance of the submarine beneath the waves. By the time he'd finished, beads of sweat were running along his neck and trickling down his back.

For several moments, the Admiral said nothing, his eyes focused on the far wall, then, rolling a black ballpoint pen between the fingers of his right hand, he asked, "Are you in the habit of risking your aircraft?"

"No . . . but since I was in the area where the *African Wolf*—"

"I am well aware of the area you were in. But are *you* aware that your fuel capacity was for a specific flight time?"

"Yes, sir."

"And you requested no permission to make the change?"

"No, sir . . . I did not."

The Admiral's face began to darken, and Healy's stomach balled into a knot. "Sir," he managed to say, "I was on that heading for not more than three minutes—"

"And in that time you alleged that you spotted a sub and made two low level passes over it?"

"Yes, sir."

"What was the lighting like?"

"Predawn grayness on the surface but with enough light to see . . . With all due respect, sir, the photographs will verify my sighting."

"I am sure they will, Lieutenant," the Admiral responded. "I am sure they will . . . but I would much prefer that they wouldn't."

"Sir?"

The Admiral looked straight at him suddenly, his eyes narrowing. Healy shifted uneasily, the movement making a squeaking noise, and reddened. Damn it, what was going on? He was angry with himself for being intimidated by the man and angry with the Admiral for not thinking he was smart enough to know what was happening. Well, he had a fair idea what would happen in Washington when the news—

"I have your Officer Personnel jacket here," the Admiral said. "From all indications you appear to be a superior naval officer."

"Thank you, sir. I hope to make the navy my career."

"I should think that an officer of your caliber would know enough not to make a course change with fuel sufficient only to get you back to the base."

"Sir, I was on a search mission, I was told to look for *any* signs of the *African Wolf.* When I saw the sub—excuse me, sir—when I saw the *alleged* sub, I immediately followed standard operating procedure."

"Perhaps so, but there are two points, Lieutenant—you might not think they're very important, but let me assure you that they are. First point . . ." The Admiral tapped the forefinger of his left hand with the end of the ballpoint pen. ". . . *You* should not have been there. Second point . . ." He moved the pen to his index finger. ". . . The *submarine* should not have been there. I have it on good authority from Naval Forces Caribbean Ops that we do *not* have a submarine in that area of the ocean. In fact, Lieutenant, there is no submarine a thousand miles from there."

The Admiral's phone rang, and with his eyes still on the junior officer, he lifted the receiver and barked, "Yes?" Then, "Send him in." He dropped the receiver back into its cradle as the door opened. "Lieutenant Healy, this is our base intelligence officer, Lieutenant Commander Thomas Cob."

The two men shook hands and Commander Cob settled himself in the chair on the right-hand side of the desk. He carried a nine-by-twelve manila envelope in his left hand.

Healy had met Cob before, a soft-spoken man with a long, sad face who lived on base with his wife. She was the reason for the face. A good-looking redhead, she reputedly drank a lot and screwed a lot.

"The photographs you took, Lieutenant, are being processed," Cob said, "but until we have them, I would like you to look at some pictures of submarines and show us which one you think you saw."

Healy nodded.

Cob carefully opened the envelope and withdrew half a dozen photographs. Handing them to Healy, he said, "Take your time. I want you to be absolutely sure of the one you select."

Healy glanced at the Admiral, who was rolling the pen between his fingers again and staring at the wall with even more intensity than before. Healy would have given a month's pay to know what was going on in the man's head.

Suddenly, Tunner said, "Get on with the ID, Lieutenant. Get on with it!"

Hastily, Healy looked down at the photographs. The first was a broadside view of a Polaris, the second an aerial shot of a conventional boat, World War II vintage . . . probably the Gatto class . . . and then the third one stopped him. He picked it up. "This is it."

"Did you look at *all* of them?" the Admiral asked, his grayish-green eyes looking hard at him.

"No, sir," Healy said. "I don't need to. This is identical to the sub I saw." He was damned if he was going to let Tunner intimidate him.

"Are you quite sure?" Cob asked.

"The photographs I took—"

"Lieutenant . . . you have just identified a modified version of our IV Poseidon submarine," the Admiral said.

"Then that's what I saw," Healy insisted. "These bubbles on the sail are the same." He pointed to the blister-like protuberances in the picture.

The Admiral glanced quickly at Cob.

"Well, we have a definite problem, Lieutenant," the intelligence officer said. "Only two of our submarines were equipped with those particular bubble sensors . . . the *Bluefin* and the *Barracuda* . . ."

"But the *Barracuda* went down in the Pacific three months ago with all hands," Healy said, surprised.

"That's right. And the *Bluefin* is on station five thousand miles from where you saw this submarine."

Healy was really sweating now. If the photographs failed to come out or show the sub with any clarity, he had only his own word to go on . . . and right now he had a feeling his word wasn't worth much. He took a ragged breath.

"Can you tell us anything more?" Cob asked.

"My radio conversation with Chief Monte and with the duty operations officer is on tape."

"Yes, I've already listened to it . . ." Cob looked at the Admiral and said, "I've arranged to give CPO Monte a two-week leave with explicit instructions to maintain *absolute* silence about this entire incident."

The Admiral nodded approvingly. "But if it takes two weeks to find out what's going on, it may be too late to do anything about it. What about the operations officer?"

"Lieutenant Commander Riggs has been temporarily assigned to the carrier *Saratoga*," Cob replied. "He's also been told to remain silent."

Healy's throat tightened and he felt his lips getting dry. He tried to clear his throat and began to cough.

The phone rang.

"Probably the photo lab," Cob said. "I left word to call me here as soon as they had something." Tunner listened a moment, then handed the phone to Cob.

"Yes . . . very clear, you say . . . no mistake about the bubble sensors . . . thank you. Yes, thank you." Cob returned the phone to the Admiral. "The photos are clear. The Lieutenant's visual ID is confirmed."

Healy gave an audible sigh of relief.

"Then, for the time being," Tunner said, "I want the Lieutenant removed from flying status, effective *immediately,* until we have some indication of what's going on. I want him to be ready to fly to Washington at a moment's notice. Got that?"

"Yes, sir," Cob responded with a nod.

Healy started to object—he did not want to be grounded —but a withering look from the Admiral silenced him before he uttered a word.

"I'll photo fax the pictures and transcription of the tape to the Deputy Director of Intelligence," Cob said. "I want him to be thoroughly familiar with what we have before I meet with him."

The Admiral nodded and turned his attention to Healy. "You may go, Lieutenant. The rest of our discussion does not concern you. But, as I said, I want you to hold yourself ready to leave on a *moment's* notice. You will keep the OD informed of your whereabouts on a twenty-four-hour basis. Is this clear?"

"Yes, sir," Healy said, relieved to be on his feet again.

"This entire matter is as of this moment top secret," the Admiral emphasized. "Any breach of security will be dealt with in the strictest possible manner."

"I understand," Healy answered, and left the office as fast as he could. Once outside, he suddenly felt as if he were going to pass out. Without bothering to glance at the Wave, who was staring at him again, he made straight for the men's room, where he was promptly sick.

"Well, Tom, what's your assessment?" Tunner asked, once Healy had gone, pushing back his chair and walking over to the window.

"I think it's fairly plain there *was* a sub out here and since it's not the *Bluefin* and it can't be the *Barracuda* . . . it's got to be one of theirs modified to duplicate one of ours. No matter how you look at it, it comes up trouble."

"What about Healy?"

"He did a damn fine job—but just so we know something more about him, I've ordered a security check. I don't think he'll be a security risk."

The Admiral didn't answer.

"I'll be leaving here about 1300," Cob said. "I have a 1600 appointment with Captain Nathan Richard."

"Healy would never have spotted the sub," Tunner said suddenly, turning from the window, "if he had stayed on his original flight plan."

"Lucky he took some initiative," Cob replied, "or we'd have an unknown sub prowling around—a sub that looks like one of ours."

"Yes." The Admiral returned to his desk. "I've already ordered four Orions to scout the area. Each ASW officer aboard has orders to report any contact directly to me."

"Do they know what they're looking for?"

"No. Just a routine exercise, they think."

"What about surface ships?"

The Admiral waved the question aside. "I don't want to blow this up out of proportion. If it's not handled right, the whole damn country will be on red alert."

"I guess you're right," Cob said. "I wonder . . . do you suppose there's any connection between that tramp, the *African Wolf,* and the sub? Maybe the freighter was sunk by her. We know from the May Day there were at least two explosions—"

"No sub captain would sink a ship and then wait around in the same vicinity," Tunner answered, shaking his head.

"Unless he was expecting to make some sort of a rendezvous and couldn't break radio silence."

Tunner was on his feet again. "Speculation!" he said angrily. "Goddamn it, we've got more than enough to explain as it is—and I suggest we start *trying* it explain it with some facts."

"Yes, sir." Cob started to gather the photographs together and replace them in the manila envelope. "I'll get started right away. If anything important develops, I'll call you tonight, or speak with you on the radio scrambler."

"I'll be at home all evening," Tunner said. "Have a good flight to the mainland—and send my best to Richard. We met once or twice when I was stationed in Washington."

Cob stood up and walked slowly to the door. "You know," he said before leaving, "if the Russians or the Chinese are going to try something, they're going to have to do it pretty fast, within the next few days. Whatever the mission of that sub is, they know they've been spotted. That fact alone is going to force their hand . . . either speed up their timetable or abort it completely."

"And we still have people who push for the SALT agreements," Tunner said with disgust. "I wonder if all those kind souls crying for detente out there would still want it if they knew there was a Russian sub prowling around our coast with enough nukes to take out every major city in the country?"

Cob didn't answer. After a moment, he said, "Let's just hope we're wrong."

The Admiral looked at him but said nothing.

Cob shrugged and left the office, closing the door softly behind him.

The hotel room overlooked the ocean. A man in his early thirties stood just inside the terrace and looked at the ocean smashing itself against the rocks. He was of medium height, broad-shouldered and fair complexioned, and dressed casually in blue slacks and a white polo shirt.

So far his stay in San Juan had been uneventful. Another day and he'd be able to enjoy himself. Two days of being holed up in a hotel room, even if it was "deluxe," wasn't his idea of fun. Without a broad or anyone else to talk to, it seemed a helluva long time.

He flicked a half-smoked cigarette over the side of the terrace and was about to walk back into the room to pour himself another shot of Old Turkey when the phone rang. In three long strides he was at the phone. Carefully, he drew up a chair, set a pad and a pen nearby and let the phone ring six more times before picking it up. He remained silent.

"We have a red situation," the voice on the other end said.

The man in the hotel room picked up the pen.

"Copy," the voice on the other end said. "Lieutenant Commander Thomas Cob departs for Washington at 1300 hours. CPO Dominic Monte departs for a two-week leave. He will be at Fifty-four twenty, Sixty-ninth Street, Brooklyn. Lieutenant James Healy lives at Twenty-eight Las Palmos, Santurce. And Lieutenant Commander Riggs is assigned TDY to the carrier *Saratoga*. Will travel to Rome via Pan Am, flight 219 out of JFK on Thursday from Rome to Gaeta by rail. When condition is green, phone the following number in Washington . . . three zero two—five three two one."

The message was repeated again while the man in the hotel room checked what he had written. There were no mistakes.

"Copied," he said and set the phone down. He removed the page with the notes, tucked it securely away, then tore off the following five pages, ripped them up and flushed the bits of paper down the toilet. Then he began to undress, pulling the uniform of a Marine flyer with the rank of major out of the closet. After putting it on and checking the way he looked in the mirror, he filled his wallet with the necessary ID papers and base ID card, complete with his photograph. He was now, as far as anyone would ever know, Major Paul Sanders, USMC.

Before he left the room, he removed an attaché case from the closet, opened it and took out a sterling silver pen, slipping it inside his shirt pocket; then, closing and locking the attaché case, he returned it to the closet.

A short while later, he stepped out of the elevator into the bustling hotel lobby. He went directly to the row of phone booths, settled into one and dialed Flight Service at Roosevelt Roads.

"This is Major Sanders," he said. "I wonder if you could get me on a 1300 flight to Washington . . . Yes, I will stop by to present my travel orders. To expedite matters, I suggest you phone Admiral Tunner . . . Yes, that's correct. I'll hold while you do it . . . Thank you."

Major Sanders let his eyes rove around the portion of the lobby in his line of sight . . . there were several very good-looking women near the desk. Too bad he didn't have any time for them now—"Yes, hello?"

"Major, your flight is confirmed," the Wave on the other end said. "You will be flying with Lieutenant Commander Cob."

"Thank you, I'll be by within the next hour or two to present my travel orders," he said, hung up, left the phone booth and went into the coffee shop for a sandwich before riding out to the base.

IV

Thursday, November 16th
1200

Major Sanders ate a light lunch: a scoop of chicken salad on a bed of lettuce, four pieces of pineapple and one slice of lightly buttered toast. He ate slowly, chewing every mouthful, thoughtful.

The only one who would present any problem was Riggs; the rest were easy, but Riggs would have to be attended to before he boarded the carrier and that meant somewhere between JFK and the base at Gaeta. To cover himself,

Sanders decided to have Riggs and Monte taken out by other operators. Yes, that would do it. Divide the labor.

He drank two cups of coffee, collected his check, then went to the desk clerk to inform him he was checking out. While the clerk prepared the bill, Sanders returned to the row of telephone booths, and put through a call to New York.

A woman answered. "Scarboro and Henderson, Business Consultants."

"This is Mister Harris, Mister James Harris. Would you please put me through to Mister Henderson," Sanders said.

"I am sorry. He's in conference and left word not to be disturbed."

"I know about the conference, I was supposed to be there. Tell him that my car broke down on the Jersey Turnpike. I'm *sure* he wouldn't mind if you put me through to him."

"Please hold on."

Within moments a man said, "Sorry about your car, James. When will you be clear?"

"It's gotten complicated."

"Yes . . . we've been discussing the complication."

"I suggest someone else meet Lieutenant Commander Riggs, either at JFK or the DaVinci Airport in Rome . . . Be sure it's someone who knows him. His flight number is 291. I can't do it and we don't want him to be alone. The same courtesy should be extended to CPO Dominic Monte, who'll be at Fifty-four twenty, Sixty-ninth Street, Brooklyn."

"An excellent suggestion," Mr. Henderson said.

"I'll be talking to you . . . By the way, as soon as one of our reps meets Riggs, have him call the home office."

"Absolutely."

The two men exchanged pleasantries, mentioned the weather and then said goodbye.

Sanders returned to the hotel desk, paid his bill, went back up to his room and a short while later hailed a cab to the International Airport on the other side of the Condado section of San Juan. At the terminal, Sanders placed his single piece of luggage in a locker, then, using the name of James Harris, went to the American Airlines counter and bought a one-way ticket to JFK on flight 720, departing at 9 P.M.

Before Sanders left the airport, he stopped at the large drugstore and purchased a cheap overnight bag and a paperback novel. He filled out the name tag on the overnight bag and, back at his locker, transferred some clothes to it from the suitcase.

At ten minutes after twelve, Sanders was picking up his travel orders at Roosevelt Roads. "You'll just about make that Washington flight," the Wave at the desk told him.

"I'm on my way," he answered with a big smile and hurried out of the room.

The C-9 was just being fueled when Sanders arrived, but they waved him aboard. Cob hadn't arrived yet and the maintenance crew was still making checks of various kinds in the cabin, so Sanders carefully took a window seat just forward of the port wing, a vantage point that gave him a clear view of anyone coming aboard.

When no one was watching, he removed the pen from his pocket, twisted the cap around four times and wedged it between his seat and the adjacent one.

Just as the fuel trucks were pulling away, the pilot and copilot came aboard and went directly into the cockpit.

Sanders saw the pilot speak to the crew chief and then to the copilot. A moment later, a staff car drove up and a tall, thin man got out.

Taking out the paperback he had bought at the airport, Sanders began to read. He suspected Cob would not be the sociable kind and would want to sit some distance from him, and he was right. Cob came aboard, saw the other officer, nodded at him and immediately went aft.

The copilot came out and asked for their travel orders.

Sanders showed his set, but Cob just identified himself and asked to be told the ETA at Washington as soon as it was established. "I'll have some radio messages to send," Cob told him.

"Yes, sir," the young officer replied.

In a few minutes, the pilot came on the PA system and asked the two passengers to obey the no smoking sign and to fasten their seat belts. The door was shut and locked. The landing steps were eased away and within moments the high-pitched whine of the jets filtered into the cabin. Vibrating and lurching, the aircraft began to move out toward the runway.

Sanders looked at his watch. The time was 1303.

Suddenly the engines stopped and the plane came to a halt.

"Major Sanders," the pilot said, over the PA system, "you have an emergency change of orders. There is a jeep on the way to pick you up."

Sanders looked out of the window. He could see the jeep racing toward the plane.

The copilot came out of the cockpit, unlocked the door and swung it open. A stairway automatically came out of the doorway. Sanders pretended confusion. As the jeep pulled up, he dropped down from the plane and raced for the vehicle.

"Go!" he ordered as soon as he was settled next to the driver.

The door on the jet closed and the ship taxied out on the runway.

"Goddamn," Sanders said, "I left my bag on the plane!"

"Don't worry, sir," assured the Marine at the wheel of the jeep. "They'll fly back tonight or tomorrow . . . You tell the Ops officer and he'll radio them."

Sanders looked at the C-9 on the runway and ruefully shook his head. "There she goes," he said. He watched as the plane rolled down the runway, gathered speed and left the ground at its characteristic steep angle. For a moment everything was silent . . . then suddenly the sky erupted in a tremendous explosion. Where the plane had been only moments before burned a huge orange ball of flames.

"Holy mother of God!" the driver said, slamming on the brakes.

The orange ball continued to hurtle forward, then exploded again, to turn to deepest red. Bits of black metal began to drop to the ground. The burning plane took a steep drop and came down at the edge of the base, slamming into an abandoned building with a roar.

Fire engines and ambulances raced toward the flames and the spewing column of thick, black smoke, but it was obviously hopeless. Nobody could be alive in there.

The driver looked at the officer next to him almost in awe.

"Luck," Sanders muttered in an awestruck tone himself. "Can you believe it? . . . Nothing but dumb incredible luck!"

At 1300 hours, Captain Nathan Richard, Deputy Director of Naval Intelligence, was informed by his secretary, Donna Mathews, that a packet marked TOP SECRET had just arrived from the communications center.

"Bring it in," he told her over the intercom. "But I'm not expecting anything." He began gathering the papers he would need for the meeting scheduled for 1330.

Richard was an early selectee for captain, forty years old, a half inch shy of six feet, broad-boned—he had to work at keeping his weight down—with brown hair just beginning to gray, a strong jaw, sensual lips and dark brown eyes. His wife, Joan, had been killed in an auto crash just one day before their fifteenth wedding anniversary, but he still kept her picture on his desk. His ten-year-old son, Henry, lived with Richard's mother and father in Kew Gardens, Queens. The boy's photograph was opposite his mother's. He looked more like her than his father. For the past two years Richard had lived alone, in a small apartment in Falls Church, Virginia, burying himself in his work.

The door opened and Donna came in. She was a lovely looking black Wave, but Richard had never been tempted to ask her out. He didn't believe in office affairs. "You have a meeting at 1330," she said, handing him the packet.

"This time I remembered, Donna." He smiled. "See, I've been gathering those papers I might need . . . but thanks for reminding me."

"Anything that should have been done yesterday?" she asked.

"No—but tomorrow, you can bet on having something that should have been done today."

She laughed and left the office.

30

Richard slit open the package and scanned the decoded message from Lieutenant Commander Cob.

From: *Lcdr T. Cob*　　　　　　　*Nov. 15*
　　　　Base Int. Officer　　　　　*0930*
　　　　Roosevelt Roads, PR.

　To:　*Captain Nathan Richard*
　　　　Dep. Dir. NavIntcom
　　　　Wash. D.C.

　Re:　*UnId Sub.*

On routine mission. Lt James Healy sighted unknown sub. Visual contact and photo ID positive. Will leave at 1300 for conf w/u. Sub can not be ID one of ours. Enc photos and transcript of tape conversation betw/pilot and base rad/op.

Richard had been a submarine commander before being assigned to intelligence, and as he examined the photos attached to the message, he immediately recognized the *Bluefin.* He made a mental note to check the *Bluefin*'s station for himself, though he was sure Cob had already done it.

The intercom buzzed.

"Yes, Donna?"

"Your meeting has been pushed up by fifteen minutes."

"Any particular reason?"

"A phone call from the chief's office," she answered.

"I'm on my way." Richard put the photos, Cob's message and the transcript back into the envelope and locked them carefully in his wall safe. He was glad Cob was on his way. What in hell was a sub like the *Bluefin* doing out there? Racing now, he picked up the papers from the desk, jammed them into a black zipper portfolio together with a yellow, legal size pad, and finally took off for the meeting at a near-run.

Suddenly he stopped and hurried back to his office. "Donna, find out what time a special flight from Roosevelt Roads will be landing at Andrews AFB, and send a car there to pick up Lieutenant Commander Thomas Cob. Have the Commander brought to my office and see if he needs anything . . . I don't know how long this meeting will last."

"I'll take care of him," Donna said, with obvious enthusiasm.

Richard gave her a questioning look.

"He's a sweet man," she said, adding after a moment, "I've known him for a while."

"Donna, you continue to surprise me. Well, then, I'm sure he *won't* need anything . . . but, Donna—I'd appreciate it if you got those reports done while I'm gone, if you can tear yourself away."

She nodded. "I thought this day was too easy to be real."

"It's real, honey," Richard said, on the run again. "Believe me, it's too real."

He arrived at the conference room just as the door was being closed by a Marine guard. A half dozen staff officers were already at the table, each one armed with a portfolio of papers and a pad for notes. At either end of the table stood a coffee carafe, surrounded by plastic cups, a small metal creamer and sugar bowl and blue plastic spoons.

Richard sat to the right of Rear Admiral Bruce Hopper, Director of Naval Intelligence and his superior. Hopper was a compact man with iron gray hair and green eyes, a veteran of the Philippines, Korea and Vietnam, and the department's most fluent linguist. Once he'd cracked a Chinese code even the State Department specialists had given up on.

Hopper nodded at Richard now and in a conversational tone, said, "I thought that by making the meeting fifteen minutes earlier, Captain, you would somehow manage to arrive on time."

"That's exactly what I thought," Richard answered. "But as you see, sir, it just didn't work out that way. If I may respectfully suggest, sir, the next time a scheduled meeting is either advanced or put back perhaps you could allow for a certain degree of tardiness for the officers who attend the meeting."

Several of the younger officers at the table had difficulty keeping the smiles from their faces—but so, for that matter, did Hopper. He enjoyed chiding Richard for his almost constant lateness, even to dinner or cocktails, but he was very fond of his deputy.

"I will keep your suggestion in mind, Captain," he said, and then, in a much more formal tone, officially opened the meeting.

Strictly as a matter of precaution, Richard checked the notes on Hopper's pad. Another of Hopper's attributes was a disconcerting ambidexterity—but he only wrote with his left hand when he was angry. By checking the slant of his writing, you could always tell his mood—and today Hopper seemed content enough. Richard settled back.

The usual format for the daily meeting was for each officer to present an update on the military condition in a particular area of the world, with special emphasis on the naval aspects of the situation. Much of it sounded routine, but then again, most intelligence gathering and assessment *was* routine. The cloak-and-dagger stuff was mostly for spy novels . . .

The meeting droned on. Admiral Hopper was very concerned about the increased presence of Russian warships in the Indian Ocean.

"In the last two weeks," he said, "they have added two more missile frigates, the *Tupolev* and the *Kaskori.* Each is equipped with—Richard, what are the specifics on those ships?"

"The *Tupolev* is seven thousand five hundred tons," Richard said, without consulting his papers. "Carries three batteries of surface-to-surface missiles and two ASW batteries, plus four surface-to-air batteries. Two of these are new and fire heat-seeking missiles . . . The *Kaskori* is ten thousand tons and is similarly armed, though she carries two more batteries of ASW missiles."

Hopper nodded and turned his attention to Rear Admiral Stanley Hays, Deputy Commander of Submarine Operations. "I want to know the position of those Russian ships on a twelve hour basis," he said. "Our subs should be able to give us that info."

Hays nodded.

One of the staff members, Captain William Gray, reported that thus far nothing further had been heard from the freighter *African Wolf.* "She is presumed lost with all hands somewhere northwest of fifteen degrees north lat., fifty-five degrees west long.," he said. "The Coast Guard called off its search at 1500 yesterday. But we had one plane in the air early this morning out of Roosevelt Roads . . . I should have an update for tomorrow's meeting."

Richard wrote the name *African Wolf* on his pad. He should ask Cob about that: was the plane mentioned by

Gray the same one that spotted the submarine?

The reports went on. At one point, Hopper nailed Captain Donald Carrs, Deputy Director for the Mediterranean Area, with a comment: "We don't seem to have a clear idea of the effectiveness of the Israeli use of high speed naval craft against PLO coastal units," he said. "Why is this? I should think we might pick up some valuable lessons from the operations, Captain Carrs."

Carrs was sitting in for his chief, who was down with the flu, and looked markedly uncomfortable. Flushing, he managed to answer, "The tactics have been hit and run, sir. It is hard to make any assessments from aboard the craft and our contacts with the PLO are very limited at this time."

"Why can't we fly recon missions during or direct after the attack?"

"Excuse me, Admiral," Richard said, "but the Israelis have not been willing to give us advanced information. I think we might speak with the State Department people to intercede with—"

"Yes, Captain, you're right, I will speak with them. It's my opinion, gentlemen, those high speed attack craft will play a very important role in future naval operations, a very important role."

Richard moved his eyes toward the window. The sky was a dull November gray that held promise of rain, or perhaps even snow. "I don't think we've overlooked anything," Hopper said.

"No, sir." Richard was anxious to return to his office and look at the material from Cob before meeting him.

"Are there any questions?" Hopper asked.

There were none.

"Then as of 1530," Hopper said, glancing at his watch, "I adjourn this meeting. Tomorrow's meeting will be held at 1400."

There was the scraping of chairs and the sound of conversation as the officers left the room, some hurrying home, others to their offices.

Richard wondered whether he should mention the unidentified sub to Hopper but decided to wait until he had more information from Cob, or at least until he had had the opportunity to review the material from Roosevelt Roads. As he gathered his papers together, his eyes rested for a moment on Rear Admiral Hays, talking to Captain Gray on the far side of the room. With a grin, Richard realized Hays had done an unprecedented thing today: not once during the entire meeting had he complained about having too few submarines in his sector of operations. He glanced at Hopper and wondered if the chief had caught it, too.

Just then, Hays and Gray were joined by Captain Robert Korman, Executive Assistant to the Deputy CNO for Air Warfare. Korman did not look at all happy, and after a muttered conversation, the three of them headed for the door. Richard was about to intercept them to find out what was wrong when Hopper called to him.

"Peggy asked if you would join us for dinner tonight," Hopper said as they strolled out of the room.

"I'd like to," Richard answered, "but I have a late conference."

"Now, Captain Richard," Hopper said, with a slight grin, "you know that my wife won't rest until she sees you married—don't ask me why, because I sure as hell won't be able to answer you—and, well, she has some pretty young candidate coming for dinner and she thought that maybe she'd match the two of you."

Richard laughed.

"Oh, Peg knows you're always being invited to parties and that you don't really lack for playmates. But she somehow feels that you'd be happier with one than many."

"I'm not so sure she's wrong," Richard replied. "But a man must make do with what a man can get."

"I'll tell her the first part of what you said," Hopper said. "But I'll leave the second part alone. Why disillusion her?"

They stopped in front of the Admiral's office. "Tell me, Captain, are you going to be spending Thanksgiving with your son?"

"Yes, but I'm not sure whether I'll go to Connecticut, or have him come down here."

"Damn fine boy," Hopper commented with the enthusiasm of a man whose only son had been killed in Vietnam. "Damn fine boy!"

"Thank you very much, sir . . . I think so, too."

"Say," Hopper began, his eyes suddenly flashing, "did you notice that Hays didn't sing his same tune at the meeting?"

"I was wondering whether you'd noticed it," Richard said.

"Let's hope it's the beginning of an era of silent acceptance." Hopper laughed. "Though I doubt it. I've known Hays a long time. Once he gets hold of something, he never lets go."

"Maybe you've finally just worn him down," Richard said. "Anyway, one more thanks to give with the turkey next week."

Hopper nodded, and with a broad smile opened the door to his office.

"Anything?" Richard asked, as he hurried past Donna.

"Admiral Tunner, base CO at Roosevelt Roads, phoned," she told him. "He said it was urgent."

"Will you get him for me?" Richard called as he settled down at the desk. In a moment his buzzer sounded.

"Admiral Tunner on four."

Richard punched at the illuminated button with his forefinger. "Captain Richard."

"Thank you for returning my call," Admiral Tunner said.

Something was wrong. There was a strange tone to Tunner's voice. For no reason at all, Richard's heart began to race and he glanced out the window. A gloomy twilight had settled over everything outside. The roadway lights were already on and in the distance he could see the headlights of the cars on Davis Highway.

"I'm afraid I have bad news, Captain," the Admiral continued. "Lieutenant Commander Cob is dead. His plane exploded and burst into flames on takeoff . . . There were no survivors."

Richard put his hand over the mouthpiece and took a deep breath.

"I know you were expecting him," Admiral Tunner said. "I wanted you to hear about the accident from me before someone else told you. I'm very sorry."

"Thank you, sir."

"If I can be of any help, don't hesitate to call on me. Naturally I am aware of his reason for wanting to meet with you. He was very concerned about what turned up in our backyard, so to speak . . . I assure you the sub was not one of ours. Furthermore, there have been no other contacts, visual or otherwise."

That meant ASW units had been sent into the area and had found nothing. Forcing himself to business, he started to ask about the *Bluefin*—

"Captain, as soon as I heard the report, I checked with Fleet Ops," Tunner said. "The *Bluefin* is a good five thousand kilometers from where the sighting took place. It is *not* one of ours."

"Did Cob say anything else to you that might give us some help?"

"Nothing."

Richard ran his hand over his chin, rough with the day's growth of stubble, then glanced down at his pad. The name of the freighter that had sunk glared out at him. "Do you think there might be some connection between the *African Wolf* and our unknown?" he asked.

"Captain, have you gone over the transcript of Lieutenant Healy's tape?" the Admiral replied, after a moment of hesitation.

"Sir, I was in a meeting from 1330 until about ten minutes ago, and Cob's packet came up from com center just before I left. I had enough time to scan the photos and that's all." He was annoyed about having to explain himself. "I know we had a plane in the area where the *African Wolf* last reported her position—"

"Yes, Captain. The pilot of that plane not only spotted the wreckage of the *African Wolf,* but made a visual contact with the unknown."

"I'll want to question him," Richard said.

"I have already taken measures to ensure he will be at your disposal."

"Thank you."

"Is there anything else I—"

"Excuse me, sir, besides Cob and the plane's crew, was anyone else aboard?"

"Yes, a Marine major by the name of Paul Sanders. Sifting through the wreckage, some of our people came up with bits and pieces of his overnight bag . . . but the bodies will take a while to sort out and identify."

Richard jotted down the major's name. "I would appreciate the full report on the crash as soon as it is available—no, I want all the interim reports as well."

"I don't see why—"

"Sir, I really would appreciate those interim reports," Richard said, knowing that under the circumstances Tunner would interpret his request as an order from Admiral Hopper.

"Very well. I will send them," the Admiral said frostily.

Richard thanked him and suggested they keep in close touch until the situation became clearer.

"I intend to, Captain Richard. Goodbye."

Richard set the phone down and glared at it for several seconds. He knew he may have made an enemy of Tunner and a man like Tunner had many, many friends in and out of the service. Tunner could send out the word about him and they would become his enemies without ever really knowing why, or still worse, without caring . . .

He did not have time for that now.

V

Thursday, November 16
1600

    Richard did not approve of anger either in himself or in others, so he let his annoyance at Tunner go and turned his attention to the problem of the submarine: first, whose was it? Second, what was it *doing* there? Reaching for a pipe, he filled it with a blend of tobacco from Wilkes in New York, lit up, and sat back in the swivel chair to think.

    Suddenly he remembered the car and driver waiting for Cob at the airport. Leaning forward, he buzzed Donna and told her to phone the SP OD at the airport to have one of the men on duty tell the driver to return to the motor pool.

"Has Commander Cob changed his plans?" Donna asked.

"Come into the office," he said, "after you finish making the call." He settled back in his chair and puffed hard at his pipe. The situation was serious. Within the next hour or so, Richard was going to have to bring the unknown submarine to his chief's attention and Hopper in turn would have to activate a yellow alert, a status condition that would affect every aspect of the nation's military machine. He felt himself beginning to sweat.

A soft knock on the door interrupted his thoughts. "Come in," he called.

Donna entered the room and came up to the desk.

"Sit down," he said, gesturing toward the chair at his right.

"I don't think I'm going to like this . . ." she murmured.

He took a deep breath and told her what had happened to Cob's plane.

For a moment, nothing happened, and then Donna's jaw trembled and the tears started to stream down her face. "Oh, God . . . Tom . . . I can't . . . it's so horrible . . . he was such a decent man . . ." She hunched over and sobbed quietly.

Richard handed her a tissue, feeling horribly awkward. "I'm sorry, Donna . . . I don't know what to say."

"Oh, please," Donna said, straightening up. "I didn't mean to bother you. I . . . He was so sweet . . . but he was married . . . We never could force ourselves to look at the future . . . I guess all that's taken care of now . . ."

"Why don't you go home now, Donna. Get yourself some rest."

"Thank you."

"And if you don't feel up to coming tomorrow—"

"No, I'll be here."

He nodded and in a few moments was alone again. Almost at once his thoughts returned to the unidentified submarine.

Relighting his pipe, Richard jotted Cob's name down on his pad, then went to the safe for the packet of material the Commander had sent him. Returning to the desk, he picked out the transcript of the conversation between the pilot, the base radio operator and the base Ops officer and read it, and then read it again. No question, the lieutenant had followed SOP, though Richard was sure that change of course to a heading of 014 degrees had not been on the original flight plan.

He added the names of the radio operator and the Ops officer to the pad, then spread out the photographs on the floor of his office. Later he would turn them over to the lab for a detailed analysis but right now his previous experience as a submarine commander gave him a good understanding of what had happened. For whatever reason the sub had been caught on the surface, it was obvious its CO had made the best possible use of natural lighting to camouflage his craft. If the RF4 hadn't gone down to photograph the debris from the *African Wolf,* the sub would have remained hidden in a pocket of predawn gray.

Richard walked around the photos, arranging them in sequence. There was little doubt the sub had executed a crash dive. Richard guessed there'd been no more than a few seconds between the time the men on the bridge of the sub had spotted the plane and the order to crash dive had been given—and probably no more than three or four minutes at the most between the time Healy had first spotted the sub and he'd made his second pass over it.

"Nathan," he said aloud, "this is one helluva hot potato." He sat down on the edge of the desk, letting his eyes roam over the photographs again. "If it's not one of ours," he whispered to himself, "it damn well must be one of theirs."

Without turning, he set his pipe down in the ashtray behind him. The Zurloof submarines were the only ones the Russians had that even came close to the size of the Poseidon . . . but why reproduce the blisters on the side of the sail? The Russians, as well as everyone else in the world, knew that the *Barracuda* had gone down and that the *Bluefin* was the only other American sub fitted out with blisters. There had been photographs of it in every American newspaper for days after the disaster.

There were only two possible explanations that he could think of. Either the Russians, or whoever it was, had developed similar hydrothermal instrumentation and had therefore come up with an identical outer package . . . or they were trying to start a military incident. In that case, God help them all . . .

He stood up, looked down at the photos, shook his head and again said aloud, "It has to be one of theirs." And that reality frightened him more than anything else had in his twenty years of service.

The phone on Richard's desk rang, shattering the silence of his office. He turned and picked it up. "Captain Richard here."

"This is Captain Gray," said the voice on the other end. "I have something I think you should see."

"Your office or mine?"

"I'll be over to yours."

Richard set the phone down, gathered up the photos of the phantom submarine and the transcript and put them out of sight. No sense spreading this around. Not yet. He answered the knock at the door himself.

Gray was obviously excited, his eyes seeming to dart around the room to check out the corners before he could speak.

"What's up?" Richard questioned warily.

"I got this about ten minutes ago from ComCenter," Gray said, handing him a message.

It was from Admiral Tunner, a repeat, essentially, of Cob's early communiqué. But what was Gray doing with it? Richard nodded, puzzled. "I was about to contact Admiral Hopper about this."

"Then Tunner sent the same message to you?" It was obvious Gray was also puzzled.

"Not exactly." Richard wanted to minimize his explanations. The fewer people who became involved with the matter, the better, at least for the present. He forced himself to appear almost nonchalant. "For now," he said, "let's say that we appear to have a problem on our hands."

"Well, what the hell are we going to do about it?" Gray asked, his voice rising.

"As I said," Richard told him, "I'm going to try to contact Admiral Hopper." He picked up the phone and dialed the Admiral's office number. His secretary answered. "This is Captain Richard, Lucy. Is the Chief there?"

"The Admiral left a few minutes ago, Captain," she said.

"He mentioned that his wife was having some guests for dinner. I imagine you should be able to reach him in about an hour . . . no, better make it a few minutes more the way traffic is tonight."

Richard thanked her and hung up. "Hopper won't be home for another hour or so," he told Gray, who was nervously smoking a cigarette.

"I sure as hell don't want this on *my* shoulders," Gray said.

"I'll take full responsibility for the decisions."

Gray looked at him. "But aren't you going to alert—"

"No," Richard replied quietly. "I want to speak to Hopper before I do *anything* that might set wheels turning— you know what's involved once we move to a yellow alert. We've got to do it through him."

"But there's something else . . ." Gray said.

"Oh?"

"A plane went down at Roosevelt Roads. No survivors."

"I know about that, too," Richard replied.

Gray said nothing, but the left side of his face seemed to twitch. He wasn't taking the pressure at all well. Richard made a note of it for future reference.

"Is there anyone else who might have received word about the sub?" Richard asked him, realizing now that Tunner had probably notified Gray to protect himself should any questions ever arise about the incident. No doubt he had logged his phone call to Richard as well.

Gray shook his head.

I wish I could be that sure, Richard thought to himself, but he said nothing and instead refilled his pipe with fresh tobacco. "My suggestion to you," he said, lighting it, "though you're not obliged to take it, is to call it a day

... go on home. If this turns into a real flap, you'll be called, you can be sure. But in the meantime, just try to relax. I'll handle it."

Gray walked to the window. For a few moments, he stood there staring out at the rainy November night. Without turning, he said, "I'm pretty new at this kind of thing . . . I don't know how the game is played."

"We try to be as flexible as possible," Richard said.

"Flexible, yeah . . . you mean cool. But how can you be cool when—"

Richard shrugged. "For this situation," he said, "the meaning is the same. Go home, Captain. If you're needed, you'll be called."

"What about the message?"

"I'll take care of it."

Gray hesitated, then, "It's in your hands, Richard," he said.

"Do you want a receipt for the message?"

"No." Gray walked to the door. "You have my home phone number?"

"Yes. Goodnight, Captain."

Gray left the office, closing the door behind him.

Richard shook his head, then took the message Tunner had sent to Gray, put it in the packet with the photographs, and replaced all of the material in the wall safe. When he returned to his desk, he tried to phone Hopper at home, but received a busy signal.

He set his pipe down, leaned back and closed his eyes. Tunner's actions still puzzled him. Now that he looked at it again, there really was no reason to send the message to Gray. Cob's original message would have covered Tunner if he'd ever needed it.

Richard gave a deep sigh. "The ways of Admiral Tunner are indeed strange . . ." Opening his eyes, he added, *No stranger than my own.*

Before he called Hopper again, Richard decided to check out the intelligence sections of the other services. Since each service guarded its secrets from the others as zealously as it protected them from foreign agents, it was always difficult to obtain information from any of them, but Richard figured he was savvy enough at least to be able to spot any unusual activity.

Casually, he walked past the Army and Air Force intelligence centers. The night crews were on and he didn't recognize any of the officers, but there seemed no tension in the air, no indication that something important was going on. Things seemed routine over here. It was his baby.

When he returned to the office, he tried the Admiral's number again. It was still busy.

Richard looked at his watch; Hopper was still busy, damn it, and he didn't dare move without him. Rather than remain in his office and become more and more annoyed at whoever was tying up Hopper's phone, Richard decided to go out for a bite and something to drink. He could use it anyway—he'd forgotten how long it had been since he'd had anything to eat. Then he'd return and do whatever had to be done.

He phoned the OD and said, "This is Captain Nathan Richard, Deputy Director of Intelligence. If Admiral Hopper comes aboard, have him *call me* at 674–3100. That's the Grass Hut down Columbia Pike from the river entrance about two miles. And should he *phone* in, have him call me there. I should be back in about an hour." He'd try Hopper himself from the phone at the Grass Hut. Before he left the

office, Richard called the Admiral's number once more
. . . It was still busy.

Captain Gray hurried out to the parking lot. A cold,
wind-blown rain was falling, and pulling up the broad collar
of his coat, he quickened his pace. At the far end of the lot,
a black limousine sat silent, but as he approached the car,
its headlights suddenly switched on, the engine started up
and it moved slowly toward him.

He stopped.

The limousine came abreast of him, halted and the rear
left side door opened.

Gray bent down and climbed into the car. Rear Admiral
Hays was waiting for him. The Admiral leaned forward and
tapped on the glass pane that separated the front and rear
of the vehicle, and the big car moved forward.

Gray adjusted his collar and took a deep breath, taking
in the smell of rich leather. Hays's position would have
rated him such a car anyway, but this limousine was actually his. Hays came from an old, moneyed southern family
whose huge land holdings had proven to be impervious to
civil war, reconstruction, and depression alike.

"Well," Hays questioned, "did he go for it?"

"Absolutely."

"Are you sure?"

"He offered to give me a receipt for the message."

Hays nodded his head appreciatively.

The car was approaching the parking-field guard. The
driver showed his pass and gestured to the rear, and the
guard waved them through, smiling.

Hays offered Gray a cigar. "These are made in Brazil,"
he said, twirling the cigar near his ear, then moving it back

and forth under his nose. "But as good as these are, there's nothing like the Cuban stuff. We'll have those again, Captain, we'll have those again. You can take my word for it." He cut the tip off his cigar with a quick movement of his penknife and lit up with a gold cigarette lighter. He held the flame out for Gray. "I think we can be reasonably certain that Richard will not check ComCenter, can't we?"

"I think so," Gray said, blowing smoke against the window.

Hays slapped Gray's knee. "By God," he exclaimed, "I think this does call for a celebration. Tonight, dinner and drinks are on me."

"Sir, I told Richard to call me at home if anything should develop."

"Don't worry about it . . . no, don't worry about it at all," Hays said. "Everything, and I mean everything, has been taken into account, including Captain Richard."

Healy was pissed. He had just spent three hours drinking in the Green Parrot after a miserable day, and now he was going home, at least that was what he'd told the OD at the base when he'd called him. Secretly, he was not so sure he could make it without collapsing.

Healy was pissed because the Admiral had had him back at his office at least five different times that day, then, when Cob's plane had gone down, the son of a bitch had called him back *again* and held him in the office, making him feel as though he were somehow responsible for the crash.

"And then," he muttered to himself, "he brings in that Marine major. What the hell was his name? Sanper . . . Sandu . . . Sanders. That was it—Major Sanders . . . a spook if I've ever met one . . . Said one of his fly-boys spotted the same sub . . . Never saw the major before . . . Never saw him . . ."

Healy lurched to one side and almost fell off the sidewalk. He steadied himself and made a low whistling sound. "Just to make my day happier, some joker has moved my apartment, moved the whole damn building from where it used to be."

He nodded and shrugged, knowing there wasn't a damn thing he could do about it, except walk to where it had been moved.

"But," he said, waving the forefinger of his right hand at no one, "the OD isn't goin' to like it one bit . . . The OD —an' I don't care who the fuck he is—isn't goin' to take kindly to having buildings moved around . . . He won't give a crap who the mother is . . . movin' buildings is definitely against regs . . . Right? Absolutely right!"

Healy stopped and leaned against a telephone pole. The street was very dark. He turned his face up and looked at the sky flooded with stars. Then dimly, from behind him, he heard footsteps. He turned and tried to focus, but the man came running at him.

Before he could move or even call out, the knife blade entered his stomach. The tearing pain dropped Healy to his knees and a blow against the side of his head sent him sprawling into the gutter.

He could hear himself moan and he could feel someone's hands moving over his body, going through his pockets. Blood welled up in his mouth and he began to cough.

He was dropping into a long, dark tunnel . . . a 9G dive . . . he couldn't pull out . . . he was going to crash. . . .

VI

Thursday, November 16th
1930

Though the Grass Hut was close to the Pentagon, it was seldom frequented by officers, so its customers came mainly from civilian personnel employed in the area. Maybe that's why Richard liked it. There was nothing particularly outstanding about the place, though there were candles on the tables, sawdust on the floor and rattan covering its walls.

Tonight, Richard practically had the bar to himself. As he munched on pretzels and sipped his Chivas slowly, he noticed two men at the far end of the bar, one of whom he'd seen several times before there, the other one a stranger. Two of the booths were occupied by couples. A candle in a yellow glass burned close to his elbow.

The events of the last few hours had troubled him deeply. Sooner or later, if he couldn't reach Hopper, he would have to alert Admiral Dorlin, the Navy Chief of Staff, himself, and that was not a step he wanted to take. However, the idea of initiating a yellow alert appealed to him even less. He did have the power under these circumstances, but it was, in his opinion, an awesome responsibility and though he had appeared *cool* to Gray, he was becoming more and more anxious about the whole situation.

Silvester, the barkeep, came up to him and griped, "See what the lousy weather does to the business. I'm not even going to break even tonight—and the forecast for tomorrow is even worse! What's a guy supposed to do?"

Richard looked around. One of the couples in the booth had left.

"You've hardly even touched your drink," Silvester said, shaking his head. "What's a matter, don't you feel good? This crummy weather makes everyone feel lousy."

Richard agreed and, finishing off his Scotch, told Silvester to give him another and went to the telephone booth. He called the OD and asked if Admiral Hopper had phoned.

The answer was no.

Richard called the Admiral's house, and this time (hallelujah!) the line wasn't busy. After the fourth ring, the Admiral's wife, Peggy, answered. *"Hello?"* Her voice sounded strained.

"This is Captain Richard," he said. "I'm sorry to disturb

you but I must speak to the Admiral."

Peggy Hopper cleared her throat and several moments of silence followed that made Richard think they had been cut off.

"Mrs. Hopper?"

"Yes?"

"Mrs. Hopper," he repeated. "It is urgent that I speak with the Admiral."

Another few moments of silence passed. He had never known her to act that way. Usually she was very friendly . . . Richard wondered if she might be miffed with him for not accepting her dinner invitation. God, he hoped not. The very last thing he wanted to do was offend her, but in the past three months alone she *had* introduced him to four different women, all of whom were on the prowl for a husband—

Peggy Hopper came back on the line. "Ah . . . Captain Richard? The Admiral left town for several days . . . He told me to tell you that he knows about the . . . situation and there's a message for you in your office."

"Excuse me, Mrs. Hopper, but are you sure he said he *knows* about the situation?"

"Yes, I even wrote his message down."

"Did he say anything else?"

"Yes, he told me to tell you to go home and get a good night's sleep." She gave a little laugh and added, "He said you worry too much."

"Yes, well, I suppose I do . . . are you sure that was all he said?"

"Quite sure, Captain."

"Well, then, thank you, Mrs. Hopper. Sorry to have

bothered you . . . and I'm sorry I couldn't make your dinner tonight."

"Perhaps another time," she said.

"Yes, I would like that."

She excused herself and hung up.

Richard went back to the bar and rubbed his chin. He was tired, but felt somewhat relieved Hopper knew about the situation. Still, it was unlike the Admiral to tell him, or for that matter anyone else, to go home and get a good night's sleep, especially if something like this was working.

For a few moments, he considered going back to the office to read the Admiral's message, but then, with a shrug, decided not to. Hopper knew what he was doing. He'd probably just scribbled a few words telling him he'd be gone for several days. Maybe his sudden departure was even in some way connected with the unidentified submarine. He wouldn't have been at all surprised if Hopper had gone down to Roosevelt Roads for a firsthand briefing from Tunner himself.

Richard smiled to himself; sooner or later, Hopper always managed to find out about everything. The submarine would probably turn out to be the *Bluefin* after all, or a modified Russian boat that was simply off course. Whichever it was, the skipper was sure to catch all sorts of hell for letting himself be caught on the surface long enough to be photographed. That kind of mistake could easily cost him his command—in either navy.

Richard paid for his drinks, bid Silvester goodnight and, with a sense of deliverance, left the Grass Hut. Turning up his collar against the rain, which had become much heavier, he walked across the gravel-covered parking area to his car. He regretted not having had something to eat inside, but lacked the inclination to go back. Besides, there were plenty of places along the way home. There was that new steak house he had been meaning to try . . . tonight would be a perfect time to stop by, since anyone with any sense at all would be home in such miserable weather.

Easing his dark green Le Mans out of the parking lot, he made a right turn and picked up speed, turning on the defroster to get the fog off his front and rear windows. There weren't too many cars on the road and the ones that were seemed no more anxious to break speed records than he was. Snow mingled with the rain, the flakes melting as soon as they touched the windshield.

Richard switched on the radio and immediately recognized the Brahms Double Concerto, the car filling with the melancholy music full of low tones that always moved him. He found himself thinking again about his conversation with Hopper's wife. Something was very different about her voice: that strained quality . . . Mrs. Hopper was a very self-possessed woman. Had she been arguing with the Admiral? Perhaps she *was* still miffed about being stood up . . .

An overhead yellow light flashed in front of him and he slowed down for the intersection coming up. Ahead he saw a set of braking lights flare red, and he eased his foot down on his own brake, carefully bringing the car to a halt on the rain-slicked highway. The traffic light shone red.

An instant later, the back of his car was struck by another vehicle, and Richard was solidly jounced against the steering wheel.

The light changed and the cars in the other lanes moved off, but, more than a little angry now, Richard got out and walked rapidly toward the other car. With a groan, he saw they were locked together by their bumpers. He stuck his head close to the window and was about to sound off at the driver when he realized he was peering down at a woman.

She was looking up at him, her lips tight, tears streaming down her cheeks and her whole body shaking.

"Open the window," he shouted.

Two cars passed, splattering him with water.

"Goddamn it!" he yelled after them, and turned his attention back to the woman in the car. "Lower the *window*, lady."

The window came down a bit.

"I'm going to try and get us separated," he told her.

"I thought I could stop," she sobbed.

Jesus, it just wasn't his day. Richard turned away and climbing up on the snagged bumpers, began jumping on them. The back of his car and the front of the woman's began to bounce up and down, and suddenly her bumper snapped out from under his, ripping the metal strip away from the rest of the body.

"Shit!" he said, and jumped down onto the roadway to assess the damage. The bumper had been completely torn away from the left side and hung by a twisted bolt to the right. The best he could do was attempt to free the bumper completely, but after a few grunting efforts, he gave up and went back to the woman in the car.

She was still sobbing.

"I'll have to drive to a service station," he told her, "and have the bumper taken off. I guess you better follow me."

"I'm so sorry," she said. "Nothing like this has ever happened to me before."

He was too annoyed to make a reply. The woman had obviously been tailgating him. What did she expect?

"Please don't be angry," she said. "You look as if you'd like to pull me out of the car and beat me—"

"More than anger," he told her, "I'm beginning to feel very wet."

"Oh, yes, oh, I'm so sorry . . . yes, I'll follow you."

Richard returned to his car and began to drive with the bumper scraping along the road. Now and then he glanced up into the rear view mirror and saw that she was staying close behind him. He couldn't see the woman's face through the falling rain, but impressions of her glimpsed through the half-open window began to come back to him now. Very attractive, actually: full lips, high cheekbones, light brown or dark blonde hair from what he could see of it—most of it was covered with a kerchief. She didn't appear to be tall. He guessed the top of her head probably reached his chin.

The lights of a service station came into view and he switched on his signal light for a right turn. In the rear view mirror, he saw her right-turn light begin to flash red . . .

Her name was Hilary Gordon. Richard found that out when they exchanged license and insurance information at the service station . . . and now he was sitting across from her at a candlelit table in the new steak house. She had been so terribly upset about the accident that, on impulse, he had asked her to join him for a drink and quickly expanded the invitation to include dinner. She had said she had a previous engagement. He had asked her to cancel it. She had hesitated. He had urged her, she had agreed . . . he was still somewhat surprised at his own nerve. He hadn't done anything like this in years—many years. Ordinarily the women with whom he went out were introduced to him by friends, or he met them at some social function. He couldn't remember the last time he had picked up a woman.

"What are you thinking about?" she asked, with a slight smile.

"How we happened to meet," he said. He liked the sound of her voice. It was soft, but not so low that he had to strain to hear it, or make him think that she was some sort of timid creature.

She laughed. "Don't tell anyone, because they won't believe you."

"Probably not," he agreed, aware of the way the candlelight played across her face and reflected in her brown eyes.

"You're staring at me," she said.

He nodded. "Does that upset you?"

"No," Hilary said, looking straight at him. "I rather enjoy it. It's frank and I'm flattered by it."

Her response pleased him and he said so. Then he motioned to the waiter. At her request, he ordered for both of them: two small steaks, broiled medium-well, and a bottle of Villages, a red Beaujolais.

The waiter told them to help themselves to anything at the salad bar.

"I think it's kind of fun to pick and choose what I want," she said, "rather than have it given to me."

Richard nodded as they went up to the salad bar together.

They ate slowly, exchanging names, dates, information. Hilary asked him his rank.

"Captain," he said.

"That's the equivalent of a full colonel in the army. Very impressive, sir. What made you choose the Navy for a career?"

"I'm not really sure. I had an older brother who was lost at sea during World War Two . . . Anyway, when the time came for me to go to college, I somehow managed to get accepted at Annapolis and here I am. And what about you, what do you do?"

"Me? Oh, I dabble around in art history . . . Italian Renaissance art, mostly. Actually," she gave a modest grin, "I'm considered something of a specialist on the Della Robbia family . . . they were ceramists in the latter half of the sixteenth century."

"Now *that,* lady, is what I call impressive," Richard said.

"Oh, dry as dust sometimes. But tell me more about you, I mean, what kind of work do you do?"

"Nothing terribly exciting. I do a great deal of paper-shuffling."

She pointed to the badge he wore. "What does that mean?"

"Submarines. I skippered one before I was transferred to my present duty," he told her.

As their conversation moved back and forth, Richard realized she was a very good listener. He told her about his former wife, his son, and even boring dumb things like his hobbies.

They spent a long time over coffee.

For the first time in hours, Richard was at peace with himself. Hilary held his full attention.

"Haven't you ever thought about getting out of the Navy?" she asked.

"Many times. But I'll probably stay until I'm too old to be of any further use . . . Besides, what else would I do?"

"I don't know you well enough to be able to answer that."

60

"Would you like to get to know me better?"

"Yes," she replied without hesitation. "Yes, I would like that very much."

He reached across the table and, putting his hand over hers, told her, "I could pretend to stumble for words but I won't . . . I'll ask you straight out to come home with me."

"Yes," she said, with that already familiar hint of a smile about her lips.

"Another coffee before we leave?"

"No," she said. "Too much coffee at night keeps me up."

Richard nodded and, summoning the waiter, he asked for the check.

VII

Captain Paul Edwards was a heavyset, owlish looking man. He enjoyed playing poker, but somehow the weekly card game had lost its spark for him; in fact, nothing he did or saw gave him a feeling of pleasure anymore. Even his need for sex had diminished to the point where Mary, his wife for the past twenty years, had told him that very evening to seek psychiatric help. He had refused, and what had started out as a reasonable conversation had turned into a violent screaming match which had ended with him storming out of the house to go to the game.

Edwards sat at the table now with the other four players: Captain Bart Morris, whose bachelor apartment provided the place for the game; Captain John Lathrope; Lieutenant Commander Jay Stewart and Commander Peter Greely. On a sideboard sat an assortment of beer, whiskey and cold cuts, prepared by the delicatessen around the corner, and paid for by a ten-dollar levy per man.

It was obvious to everyone that Edwards was paying little attention to the game. "Listen," Morris said with his New York twang, "I don't mind taking your money, but tonight you're just giving it away. You're just not following the cards, man."

Edwards said nothing, but early in the next hand, he folded. Leaving the table, he went to the bar on the other side of the room, poured himself a double shot of bourbon, and walked to the window. Drink in hand, he stood there looking out at the street, watching the snow mixed with rain.

Behind him, the men talked about a plane that had crashed on takeoff earlier that day at Roosevelt Roads.

Greely was saying, "I don't know why, but word came down to put a security clamp on the story. I was told it came straight from Admiral Hopper himself, or at least from his deputy, Richard."

"Yeah, something's going on, that's for sure. You know, I saw Hopper myself at about 1700," Lathrope added. "He was with that stuffed shirt Crawton—retired Rear Admirals ought to *stay* retired, if you ask me—and some civilian, and Hopper looked angrier than hell."

Edwards heard the conversation but really wasn't interested in any of it. He was still upset over his argument with Mary. They had had a good life together, and though he was no Prince Charming, she loved him and he loved her. He knew that if the present situation continued, their marriage wouldn't last another three months. Mary enjoyed sex and had never been coy about it.

He lifted the glass and in one long swallow finished the drink, then returned to the bar and poured himself another. Back at the window, he saw a young woman across the court come to a window and lower the shade. Her shadow was visible as she undressed.

Edwards knew what was wrong with him and he realized that with each passing day he was drawing closer and closer to the edge of a pit. He had been that way ever since the *Barracuda* had gone down.

Edwards had designed the special instrumentation for the *Barracuda* and the *Bluefin* that monitored the thermal variations in the water surrounding the submarine, giving the skipper a constant readout of temperature differentials. With them, not only could the skipper better conceal his craft from surface and air anti-submarine units, but by using the thermal layers, he could prevent the sudden destruction of his craft by avoiding those huge currents of cold water that poured through the ocean like the torrents over Niagara Falls.

Edwards's devices should have insured the safety of the *Bluefin* and the *Barracuda,* and guaranteed that the Navy would never again sustain a loss like it did with the *Scorpion,* which had gone down several years before off the Azores. But instead they had failed. The *Barracuda* had gone down in more than a thousand meters of water with all hands lost. The Navy hadn't officially blamed him, no one *blamed* him, but Edwards knew. And now he was waiting for the *Bluefin* someday to meet the same fate . . .

Edwards bolted down his second drink and was about to get another when Stewart said, "Speaking of Crawton, another strange damn thing happened the other week. I could have sworn I saw his son, Crawton, *Jr.,* live and in the flesh, just like nothing had happened to him." Ignoring Lathrope's frantic signals, he went on, "I tell you, if ever a man had a twin, then I was looking at Captain Crawton's double. If he hadn't been in civvies and with a woman, I would have at least gone up to him."

"Will you *shut up,* Jay?" Greely said.

But it was too late. Edwards drew closer to the table. "Where?" he asked. "Where did you see him?"

"Rio," Stewart answered in a low voice, embarrassingly aware now of the mistake he had made.

"Rio," Edwards repeated. Then, looking hard at the man, "When was it?"

"Take it easy," Greely said, beginning to stand.

"I just want to know when," Edwards said.

"Ten days ago."

Edwards repeated Stewart's answer and, going to the bar, poured himself a third drink.

"Aren't you going a bit strong on the juice?" Morris asked.

Edwards lifted his glass. "No, not at all. I want to give a toast, gentlemen. A toast to Captain Crawton's double, a toast to the doppelgangers of *all* the men who were on the *Barracuda,* may they live long and useful lives . . . very long and very useful lives . . ." His voice broke and his hand trembled. The glass struck the floor and shattered.

The men at the table glanced at each other.

"Don't you see," Edwards said, "don't you see we owe it to them . . . owe it to all of the men who went down on the *Barracuda,* to all of the men I failed . . ."

Edwards sat at the kitchen table, working on his third cup of very strong black coffee, and feeling miserable. He apologized to Morris for having broken up the game. Usually it lasted until about two in the morning; it was not quite 12:30 A.M.

"The guys understand," Morris said. "Hell, they know the strain you've been under these last few months and they sympathize with you."

Edwards nodded. "I really appreciate your help. I know you've been covering for me at the lab—"

"I told you before," Morris said. "I don't want to hear about it."

Again, Edwards nodded.

"You know what would be a good idea? I think you should ask for an emergency leave and take Mary to a place where the two of you will be able to relax. Like a second honeymoon . . . get all this out of your system."

"Won't work," Edwards said, looking down into the empty cup. "It won't work." Then, moving his eyes up to Morris, he asked in a low voice, "Do you know what I mean?"

"Yes, but that's because you're under a lot of *strain.* Any psychiatrist will tell you the kind of strain you've been under would make *any* man impotent . . . It's even happened to me."

"I think I'm on the edge of a breakdown," Edwards whispered.

"C'mon, Paul, you don't really mean that."

"I wouldn't have said it if I hadn't meant it."

Morris poured him more coffee. "Look . . . sometimes this sex thing can be worked out with another woman, someone who can help you get your confidence back . . . I can fix you up with someone who goes wild in bed."

Edwards shook his head. "No . . . thanks, Bart, but no good. The transcript of the court of inquiry just keeps running through my head. It blocks out everything else. You know how good my memory's always been." He gave a short laugh. "Much help it is to me now." He closed his eyes. "Without half trying," he said, "I can see it all now, the members of the court, the details of the room . . . sitting up there, Rear Admiral Fields, Captain Howard Smith, Admiral Gregory White, Captain Richard Selby, Captain Mark Osborn . . . all of them submarine commanders, Captain Osborn from the *Bluefin* . . . For four days, the sun poured through the window during the afternoon, and I sat there . . . sat there . . ." He looked across the kitchen table and tapped the right side of his skull. "It's all up here . . . every word, every gesture of the court, and then the Senate *subcommittee* hearing."

"But why dwell on it, why whip yourself with it?"

"Because something was *wrong*—"

Morris started to stand.

Edwards's hand shot across the table and grasped his friend's wrist. "Look, Bart, will you do me a favor? This may sound crazy, but listen to this. Sit and listen to me and then tell me what you think."

Morris sat down again and said, gently, "Okay, Paul, go ahead."

Edwards withdrew his hand. "Okay . . . Now, let me run

some of the proceedings through again. There were some fifty witnesses, right? Everything about the *Barracuda* was examined."

"Yes, I remember," Morris said.

"Then I was called. I gave my rank and told them I held a Ph.D. in physics from MIT with a particular specialty in the detection of macrothermal differences in large bodies of water. I was asked to cite some of my published papers and I explained the kind of instrumentation I had designed for the *Barracuda* and the *Bluefin*. The court was pretty good up to that point, okay?

"But then Captain Adset, the court counsel, began to ask me questions. He wanted to know why a man of my *standing* preferred the Navy to working for the civilian sector, and why I had never held any sort of shipboard responsibility, and how could I design equipment without really ever having lived aboard a submarine for any length of time? . . . What it really came down to was my culpability. I was responsible for the design of an imperfect set of instruments that failed to do what I had specified they would do."

"But the court couldn't possibly know that," Morris replied.

"Right. *No one* could know that, but that didn't stop them from making certain inferences. Oh, they admitted the *Barracuda* had been ordered to maintain strict radio silence and that they did not *know* whether the instruments functioned properly or not—"

"But you weren't even cited for any negligence. Your instrument package is still on the *Bluefin* and from all the reports I've seen, it's functioning exactly as you predicted it would."

"Then what happened aboard the *Barracuda?*" Edwards

shouted, slamming his fist down on the table. "What happened aboard the *Barracuda?*"

Morris shook his head.

"Okay, now we come to the Senate subcommittee hearing, just five days after the court of inquiry. Hardly enough time for me to clear my head . . . No, wait, I forgot Crawton. Jesus Christ, how could I forget *Rear Admiral* Crawton's report to the court. I'll never know how that son of a bitch managed to get himself appointed special consultant to the court. That report of his? Four hundred pages, and you could sum it up in one word: sabotage. Spies everywhere . . . and if he didn't actually come out and say I was a spy, he came damn near close to it.

"*Then,* in the Senate subcommittee hearing, who should pick up the same cry but the *illustrious* Senator Eastham of Mississippi, the Defender of our Nation—and who joins him? Crawton! Somehow, Crawton got into those hearings, too, and the two of them turned the whole affair into a Roman circus.

"But now let me tell you what struck me a few minutes ago that somehow never really penetrated to my skull at the inquiry or the hearings. We know there are, or were, family ties between the Senator and the Admiral: the Senator's sister married to Captain Crawton's first cousin on his mother's side. And who did that first cousin happen to have been—the Exec aboard the Barracuda, Commander Tad Haywood."

"So? That's common knowledge. What does it prove?" Morris said.

"Nothing, precisely. But here we have Eastham making the most over the fact he had two relatives aboard the *Barracuda.* And then we have Crawton making brave eulogies and using the hearing as a platform for his political ambitions—can you believe he actually thinks he can be President?—and then we have . . . look, I don't know if you ever met Crawton, *Jr.,* but I had dealings with him when the two instrumentation blisters were installed on the *Barracuda.* If the father is anything like the son, he'd like nothing more than a war with Russia, or China, or *somebody* . . . Captain Crawton gave me a two-hour lecture on the need for an American preemptive strike against Russia. He may have been a damn good sub commander, but his politics . . ."

"So, what are you saying, Paul? That *Admiral* Crawton *engineered* the sinking of his son's sub to use as a propaganda platform? That's crazy!"

"No, no, no, I'm not saying that . . . I'm just saying . . . oh, hell, I don't know . . . just that *something* was wrong and *is* wrong, I just have a gut feeling about it. It's all too . . . and tonight when Stewart mentioned he saw Crawton Jr. with a woman in Rio—"

"Someone who *looked* like Crawton, Jr."

"Hell, Bart, Crawton was a cunt man. You know it, I know it, and every other damn officer knows it."

"*Was* . . . that's the key word, Paul. Was . . . he's with all the other men on the *Barracuda* now," Morris said.

Edwards shook his head. "I know something is wrong. I can't put my finger on it, but there's some connection that goes beyond the loss of the *Barracuda* and the hearings . . . I'd bet my life on it . . ."

November 16th. Ship time, 2000 hours. This is the 139th day since we were reported lost. A very disturbing incident happened yesterday. Until

1900 last night, as previously noted, all members of the crew were in excellent health. But two days ago CPO 3rd class William Pauls died after an emergency appendectomy. The appendix had ruptured before surgery. We surfaced just before dawn and held the burial at sea. The decision to surface was my own. It was done to impress upon the rest of the enlisted men the importance of our mission, though none of them have any idea what our mission is. They know only what they have been told, and they have been told only that we are on an extended patrol that will eventually take us into hostile waters.

We had just completed services and all of the enlisted men were below. I was on the bridge with Tad Haywood, my Exec, and Pete Howell, our missile firing officer, and we were just about to go below ourselves when suddenly an R4F came down at us from out of the west, where the sky was still dark. Howell started to yell and wave his arms.

I immediately ordered him to desist and the ship to crash dive, but the recon plane was able to make another pass over us as we were awash. I saw the plane through the periscope. I ordered a cruising depth of 60 fathoms and continued full speed along our predetermined course, and as soon as we were running smoothly, I summoned Steve Donaldson, our electronics officer, to give him a message to send to our command center informing them of our encounter.

The return message ordered me to proceed as planned.

From what I hear about the reaction of the enlisted men to the incident, I can safely assume they do not know we were spotted by a plane. According to Tad, the men are of the opinion that my order to crash dive was just another drill in a long list. Some of them even said they almost expected me to order something like that at a time they would least expect it.

That has been our only intercept on the mission so far, and I hope it will be the last. I must now rely totally on the people on shore to nullify my error. I should not have surfaced. The body could have been discharged through one of the torpedo tubes, but I thought I could keep the morale of the crew high by this ceremony, despite the loss of a man. There is a definite mystique about a burial at sea that binds all men together and I wanted the crew to experience some of that. There is a more pronounced separation between the officers and the enlisted men here than is usual on similar craft. I was going to add "and on similar missions" . . . but no mission has ever been, or ever will be, similar to this one.

Of the other two officers on the bridge with me, I am only concerned about Howell. The incident has definitely unnerved him. In the days to come, as we draw closer to the operational area, he will have to be watched for any signs of breakdown.

The strain on all of us is tremendous, but it must be borne if we are to be successful. . . . End of entry, Captain Crawton, commander of the submarine *Barracuda.*

VIII

Thursday, November 16th
2100

As soon as the car came to a stop, the man Crawton had called Jimmy removed the blindfold from Admiral Hopper's eyes. Hopper blinked, and tried to look around, but he could see little through the glare of the headlights reflected off the falling snow.

Hopper had been packing up to go home when Crawton and Jimmy had come into his office. Jimmy had come up to him and in a low voice said, "Admiral, there's a gun in my hand. I suggest you do what Admiral Crawton tells you to." After that Jimmy had not said another word. . . .

"This is a nice place to spend a few days," Crawton commented as he led the way toward the house.

Hopper remained silent.

The house was more of a hunting lodge than a regular dwelling. The bottom part was fieldstone and the rest made of logs. Smoke was coming out of a fieldstone chimney set in the peaked roof.

As they walked, their footfalls made a crunching sound in the snow.

Crawton opened the door and gestured Hopper in. Jimmy followed immediately behind them.

The downstairs appeared to be one big room, complete with a stone fireplace, chairs, tables, a sofa, several shelves of books, a radio but no TV. There was a kitchen off to one side. Through the open doorway, Hopper could just make out a gas range and a refrigerator. The bedrooms, Crawton explained, were upstairs.

"There's a small staff here who will see to your needs," Crawton told him. "For the next few days you will find it very comfortable here. Whatever we don't have, ask Jimmy. He'll get it, or one of the other men will. . . . Now if you will give me your hat and coat. Thank you."

Hopper remained standing in the middle of the room, near a large table, his eyes fixed on Crawton. He said nothing. He wanted Crawton to do all the talking, then maybe he'd find out why he had been kidnapped and why he had been forced to write a note to Captain Richard, explaining that he had taken the package (*what* package?). He hoped Richard would know something was wrong when he saw the note. Hopper had left the clue that he felt Richard should recognize . . .

"I'm sorry it had to come down to this," Crawton was saying. "I know you're a dedicated officer, though your politics have blinded you to the real purpose of having a strong military machine."

"Sorry?" Hopper echoed. "No, I don't think you are."

A smile flickered briefly across Crawton's lips and with a nod, he said, "You're right. I have no regrets. I'm doing what must be done to protect this nation." He spoke with the conviction of a man convinced his moment had come. Crawton was a tall man with gray, wavy hair and a ruggedly handsome face that belied his sixty-two years. He was charismatic and he knew it. "Men like us know what the real stakes are. We've dealt with reality all our lives and—"

"Please, no speeches," Hopper said.

Crawton's lips tightened. He didn't like to be spoken to that way.

"How long am I going to be your guest?" Hopper queried.

"Three, possibly four, days."

"Then what?"

"By that time, all that must be done will be done," Crawton answered with the hint of a smile.

Hopper's brows drew together . . . Could Crawton and his friends actually . . . possibly . . . be involved in some kind of crazy coup d'etat? The possibility was there, however farfetched on the surface. How many men would be killed trying to defend the government, and how many would die trying to destroy it? Where would the Navy stand? Would it follow Crawton or—

"Don't bother to try to figure it out," Crawton told him. "It is all very complex—or rather, so deceptively simple that it appears to be complex."

"You know kidnapping is—"

Crawton shook his head.

"Reasonableness," Hopper said, "was never one of your strong points."

"I hope it will be your strong point when the time comes for you to make a decision," Crawton responded. Turning, he started for the door, then stopped. "I should tell you," he said, facing Hopper, "that should you attempt to escape, you will be shot and—"

"After I'm shot, what more could you possibly do?" Hopper asked.

"Your wife will be killed too." Crawton looked straight at Hopper. "Our people are with her now and they will remain with her while you are here."

Hopper could feel his teeth gritting. But he kept silent.

"We had to take precautions," Crawton said.

"Yes, you must," Hopper agreed. "Especially when you're committing treason."

Crawton stepped rapidly back from the door, his face suddenly very red, and stopped directly in front of Hopper. "Don't talk to me about *treason,*" he said. "*Treason* has been and *is being* committed by the men who think they can live on the same planet with the Soviets and the Chinese Communists. *Treason* is doing business with them, selling them our wheat and corn, letting them buy our machinery. *Treason* is not destroying them while we have the opportunity. *That's* treason—and that's what we intend to put an end to."

"I see. And you and your friends will end it in three days,

or maybe four if the job proves slightly more difficult than you anticipated?"

"Exactly."

Hopper stood for a moment facing the red-faced man, then said, in a calm voice, "Treason, Steven, is what you are about to commit."

Crawton looked as if he was about to explode again, but instead took several deep breaths and, shaking his head, hurried out of the room.

Hopper turned his attention to Jimmy. The man looked to be in his early thirties, about five feet ten, one hundred eighty pounds. He wore a gray suit and was armed with what appeared to be a snub-nosed .38 which he wore in a black leather holster at his hip.

"Three or four days is a long time," Hopper said.

Jimmy didn't answer.

Hopper really hadn't expected him to, but it had been worth a try. He walked to the window. It was snowing heavily, but the woods were close enough to the house for him to make out the darker white trunks of several bare-limbed birches. Other than that, nothing.

He faced the room again. There was nothing he could do, except wait, and that was always the most difficult thing of all. He looked at Jimmy and was about to speak when the high-pitched whine of an automobile's wheels spinning in the snow could be heard, followed by a screech as they grabbed hold.

"Crawton's gone," Hopper said, looking toward his guard.

But Jimmy didn't answer. . . .

The two men sat in the front seat of a black Olds Ninety-eight, circling the block where CPO Monte lived. They made several passes before finally finding a parking space some distance from the two-family house but with a clear view of the stoop.

The man behind the wheel was tall and thin. His name was Hal. The one next to him, almost as tall, but much broader, was known as Stooky. Both men wore loose-fitting overcoats and broad-brimmed hats.

"Cruddy night," Hal said. "If it turns any colder, we'll have fucking snow and ice all over the place."

Stooky reached into a brown paper bag and took out a container of hot coffee, handing it to Hal. "You want a jelly doughnut or cinnamon?"

"Cinnamon," Hal said.

The two of them made slurping noises as they drank.

"What the hell is so important about this Ginzo sailor boy?" Stooky asked. "I mean, he's gotta be real important for someone to pay ten big ones for the job."

"I don't ask questions," Hal answered. "If the money wasn't good, you can bet your ass I wouldn't be sitting here."

"Are you sure he's not home?"

"Yeah, that's what his kid brother told me when I called. He said he went to visit his girl friend."

"He didn't say when he'd be home?"

"The kid didn't know."

"What if the sailor boy decides to spend the night balling his girl friend?"

"Jesus, I sure as shit hope not. I mean, hell, wham-bam, thank-you-ma'am, what more does he need?" He laughed. "No, I think lover boy will be home tonight."

The two men finished their coffee and put the empty containers and lids back into the paper bag.

"Do you suppose someone will spot us sitting in the car?" Hal asked.

"Not on a night like this. Besides, I lifted this car from a street half a mile away before I picked you up at the subway station. All we gotta do is finish the job and then dump the car . . . Bang it up a bit to make it look as if some kids heisted it and went out joy-riding."

They fell silent. Hal took out a cigar from his inside breast pocket, removed the wrapper and bit off the tip. A match flared briefly in the darkness, and Hal sat back to smoke . . . and wait.

CPO Dominic Monte walked jauntily along Eighteenth Avenue toward Sixty-ninth Street. Man, this leave had worked out even better than he'd expected. He'd been worried about his girl, Nina. Her letters to him were always talking about how all her friends were getting married, and how all the men she knew kept asking her to marry them and . . . well, Monte had gotten the message.

Unmindful of the rain, he whistled softly to himself. All it had taken was a face-to-face meeting, a little finessing, as Healy was always telling him. Not only had he managed to get laid tonight, but he'd come to a kind of understanding with Nina. They'd agreed he would buy her an engagement ring for Christmas, and if everything went all right, they'd get married the following June . . . Hell, it'd be a kick. She was great in bed, and they had a lot of fun the rest of the time, too, fooling around, being together. Yeah, it'd be all right. . . .

The way Monte figured, he would stay in the Navy for

twenty years. That meant he'd only be forty-two when he got out, and his pension would give him the opportunity to look around, decide what he wanted to do with the rest of his life. He hadn't exactly told Nina he planned to stay in the service that long . . . but he had said he didn't want to rush out into civilian life and start punching a time clock.

He wondered if he could manage another leave for Christmas. Could be . . . Commander Cob had told him this one wouldn't be counted against his accrued leave time; it was some kind of special deal, something to do with the radio conversation he had with Healy about the submarine. Cob had told him to keep his mouth shut about it, and he had.

Monte turned the corner onto Sixty-ninth Street and smiled. In two weeks or so, most of the windows along here would be decorated with Christmas lights and there would be plastic crèches in some of the gardens. Though Christmas had meant a great deal more to him when he was a kid, he still enjoyed it most of all the holidays—and not because of the religion so much . . . He just liked the idea of giving and receiving gifts.

He started to cross the street.

A black car pulled away from the curb.

Monte stopped and looked toward the onrushing vehicle. No lights . . . Jesus, it was heading for him. He tried to backstep. It cut toward him. Panicked, he started to make a dash for the opposite side. The car swerved.

He screamed as it hit him and he felt himself being tossed into the air. He dropped down on the hood, caught a glimpse of the two men behind the windshield, and rolled off into the rain-wet gutter. . . .

IX

Friday, November 17th
0100

It was snowing heavily in New York by the time American Airlines flight 720 from San Juan landed at JFK International Airport.

James Harris dashed past two other people waiting for a cab to pull in and claimed it for his own. The driver was about to object, but Harris held up a twenty dollar bill. The cabbie nodded, put his flag down and asked him where he wanted to go.

"Triple six on Madison Avenue," Harris told him, settling back.

The snow forced the cab to go slowly. Harris didn't mind the extra time. He closed his eyes and softly began to intone his mantra, willing himself into a state of relaxation. The whirr made by the cab's tires in the snow helped enclose him in a cocoon of tranquillity, and bit by bit he could feel each part of his body become limp as he went deeper and deeper into self-hypnosis.

Even in this state, however, Harris was peripherally aware of everything outside. He could hear the cabbie speak, but did not answer. He knew when they turned onto Long Island Expressway from the Van Wyck and when they entered the Queens midtown tunnel. And he was fully awake when the cab cut east on Fifty-seventh street and swung north on Madison Avenue.

A short time later he entered the building, rode the elevator up to the twentieth floor and entered the offices of Scarboro and Henderson, Business Consultants.

"May I help you?"

He told the night receptionist he wanted to see Mister Henderson.

"I'm sorry," she answered, "but he's in conference."

"I *know* about the conference," Harris said, setting down his valise. "I'm supposed to be in there, but my car broke down on the Jersey Turnpike. Please buzz me through to him."

She looked at him skeptically and, picking up the phone, dialed three numbers. "Hello? There's a Mister *Harris* here who's arrived for the conference . . . ? He is? Thank you." She put the phone down. "Mister Henderson will be out in a few minutes. Please sit down and make yourself comfortable."

Harris dropped down into a comfortable-looking, light wood, Swedish modern chair with a dark blue cushion. From his previous contacts with Scarboro and Henderson, he knew there was a staff here all night as well as all day. Most of the night people were involved with computer operations.

After five minutes, the frosted door opened and a tall, handsome man in his late fifties came into the anteroom. He held out his hand. "I was sorry to hear about your difficulties on the turnpike."

Harris was on his feet. "Those things happen sometimes," he said.

"If you will follow me."

They moved quickly past the frosted glass door and into the corridors of the offices. Neither of them spoke. Finally Henderson led him into a large room with a view of Queens obscured by the night and the falling snow. Several men were seated around a rectangular mahogany conference table.

Henderson took Harris's coat and hat and gestured for him to sit down, then went to the head of the table.

Harris nodded to several of the men. He had met them all before, except one, a thickset individual with black hair and bushy eyebrows.

"We know about the crash," Henderson said. "There was some mention made about it, but then nothing else."

"Healy met with an accident," Harris said.

"Fatal?"

"Yes."

"Good. Not too long ago," Henderson said, "I received

a phone call about CPO Monte. He was struck by a hit-and-run driver. He is not expected to live."

"That leaves Riggs." Harris turned his attention to the thickset man. Instinctively he knew they were in the same business.

"Mister Laws," Henderson said, "has run into an unforeseen difficulty."

Harris stiffened. He had no use for people who tried to excuse their lack of performance by claiming "unforeseen difficulties."

"Riggs was not on the flight to Rome," Laws said, looking straight at Harris. "He was not on flight 291."

Harris looked to Henderson. "He was booked for that flight."

"I checked all the other airlines that had flights to Rome," Laws said. "He wasn't on any of them."

"But his orders say—"

"Fortunately," Henderson interrupted, "our good friend in Roosevelt Roads was able to help us. Riggs switched flights. He managed to get three more days before reporting aboard the *Saratoga* and flew to Milan instead. He is staying at the Hotel la Scala."

"Why the change of plans?" Harris asked.

"It seems," one of the other men said, "that Riggs is something of an opera buff. He wanted to see an opera."

"An opera buff," Harris repeated with disgust. "Jesus." Then, looking at Laws, "I'll take him out."

Laws made an open gesture with his hands and looked toward Henderson.

"Are you sure you're up to it?" Henderson asked Harris.

"If I go, I know it'll be done."

"Now just what the hell do you mean by that?" Laws said, starting to rise.

"Sit down. Exactly what I said. You should have checked *all* the flights going to Italy—Rome and Milan."

"What's done is done," another man at the table commented.

"It's what *isn't* done that worries me," Harris answered coldly. "There's already been one fuck-up and now we can't have another . . . Let me remind all of you that we can't afford this. I don't know what the hell was in Crawton's mind when he decided to surface, but you can see for yourselves what the result was, and *now* we have someone loose who should have been covered."

The men at the table shifted uneasily; they had to agree.

"We only need to keep the lid on for three more days, four at the outside. After that we'll be playing a different game—*but* I don't have to remind you gentlemen what will happen if we fail."

Henderson broke in hurriedly. "I've made reservations for you at the Hotel Pierre tonight and I'll send the plane tickets to you in the morning. The La Scala booking will be waiting for you."

Harris shook his head. "*No*. I'll make my own arrangements. It's safer that way."

Henderson paused. "As you wish. Is there anything else, gentlemen?"

The men at the table shook their heads.

"I'll see you out," Henderson said to Harris.

"Don't bother," he answered. "I can find my own way."

Sometime later, Harris looked down from the window of a special company jet. The lights of New York looked like yellow diamonds strewn on black earth.

Damn their stupidity, he thought. Then he turned away from the window and thought ahead to Milan.

November 17th. Ship time 0200. For the first time since this mission began, I have not been able to sleep. I keep thinking about the recon plane. There is no doubt in my mind it must have taken photographs of us and that the pilot must have communicated with his base. I wonder if the plane's appearance had anything to do with the May Day call we picked up from that freighter four or five days ago. Strange how events can revolve on such small coincidences . . .

The question uppermost in my mind now, and in the minds of the other officers aboard, is how fast our people on shore can act to keep this operation from unraveling. So much planning and effort have been expended . . . the mission *must* be completed.

I think it can. Twenty hours have passed since we were sighted and we have traveled more than a thousand miles from the point of interception. Several times our radar has picked up planes and once, at periscope depth, I saw a single aircraft to the southwest of us that appeared to be flying a figure-eight search pattern. Even if it came closer, or flew directly over us, however, I do not think we would be in any danger of being found. The hydrothermal instrumentation in the two blisters on the sail keep us informed of the temperature differentials between the currents, and by sailing the *Barracuda* directly in the interface zone, we are effectively shielded from detection. Without this new technology we could never have hoped to carry out our plan.

We should reach our target area in another three days. Once we are in the Mediterranean the run to the Aegean Sea will be no more than another twenty-four hours. Without further mishaps, our missiles will be launched sometime on the 21st.

Except for those few days in Rio, I have spent the past three months entirely aboard the *Barracuda,* and from time to time, I have thought about my life, the events that, when added together, have inexorably moved me to where I am now.

I have previously commented about my father. Even if he were not an admiral, he would have found some way of bringing his patriotism into play, his vision of what the United States should be. And it is from him that I took my vision.

All through my life I have felt as if I somehow had a more important destiny than most other men: that something was given to me at my birth, or perhaps at the moment of my conception, that tended to set me above other men, that marked me to carry out special enterprises. To be able to fulfill that role, I have brought myself to a state of physical and mental perfection that far, far exceeds any of my officers, and they are men who are in all ways superior to the other officers in the Navy.

I was chosen for this command, not by my father, who could have done it if he had wanted to, but by a vote from the civilian arm of our organization. They examined the qualifications of several senior officers and I was selected above all of the others.

In Plato's *Republic* the citizenry are divided into categories that reflect their worth in terms of metal. Those who are worth most to the state are gold, while those who are worth least are base metals. I believe in that. I believe that some men are indeed gold and meant to lead, meant to be and have the best of everything.

All of the officers aboard this boat and all of those ashore who are part of our organization are in that category. But the real difference between us and other men is that we have a *purpose*—something to put our faith in, something we can trust and something to build for.

At one time Christianity provided such a purpose, a cause, but now we must work for something more than just belief in God. We must work for belief in the protection here and now—a pure and decent nation.

Our mission is to make the United States the only supreme world power. Once that is done, our organization will take political control—no, let me restate that. Our organization will be *given* political control by a grateful citizenry.

As all roads at one time led to Rome, all roads will now lead to Washington, and our country will garner from all other nations the tribute that will rightfully belong to it. Our cause is to restore to the United States its rightful place in history and to put those people in power whose energies will be directed to maintaining our God-given, and man-earned, superiority.

I, and those officers with me, are willing to die, if need be, to accomplish our goal.

There are, of course, those individuals who would label us fanatics and they would be right, because if a cause is truly worthwhile, then those who espouse it must be willing to give their lives for it. But if the men are not willing to make the ultimate sacrifice, then the cause itself is probably worthless. The officers on the *Barracuda* know the worth of their cause and their contribution to it.

End of entry, Captain Crawton, commander of the submarine *Barracuda*.

Admiral Crawton was glad to be home. The day had been grueling and the fight with Hopper had left him exhausted. Though he had always thought Hopper a political idiot, he could not help admiring the man's ability as an officer. He regretted having had to kidnap him, but he had had no choice under the circumstances. The man was too clever.

As the car turned on to his street, Crawton sighed deeply and moved slightly forward. A few moments later the vehicle swung into a driveway and came to a stop in front of an English Tudor-style house. The chauffeur immediately went around to the other side of the car to open the door for Crawton.

"You might as well stand by tonight," Crawton told him. "I don't know what might happen."

The man nodded.

Crawton walked slowly toward the house. Snow was still falling. It had already covered the garden and coated the bare limbs of the trees.

Before Crawton reached the door, the butler opened it, and the Admiral handed him his coat and hat. "I will be in the study," he said. "Have cook fix me a bowl of soup and—"

"Sir, you have visitors," the butler said.

Crawton frowned, then raised his eyebrows questioningly.

"The Senator and his associate, Mr. Robert Gibbs."

Crawton nodded. The Senator could only be Eastham and Gibbs was a Company man. Crawton had met Gibbs several times while he was arranging for the sale of a World

War II, Gato-class submarine to the Chilean government for underwater research and development. Gibbs had not only been indispensable in that effort, he had since coordinated a great many other activities between Crawton's group in the Navy and Company people who had similar ideas.

"How long have they been here?" the Admiral asked.

The butler glanced at the grandfather clock against the opposite wall. "Since about midnight," he said. "I took the liberty of serving them coldcuts and drinks."

Crawton nodded approvingly.

"I also had their car placed in the garage."

Crawton thanked him, shook the weariness from his shoulders, and walked into his study, closing the door behind him.

Eastham was a heavyset man with a jolly face and thinning gray hair who had comfortably ensconced himself in a wingback leather chair in front of a roaring fire. He must have dozed off for a moment because when Crawton entered the room, he looked startled and scrambled to his feet.

Gibbs had not been dozing. He stood on the far side of the room, in front of the ceiling-to-floor bookcase, and turned now. "I was admiring your books," he said. "A fine collection." Gibbs was slender and not quite six feet, a very different sort of physical specimen from either the Senator or Crawton. His brown hair was very light, and his green eyes and heavy lips served to accent his high cheekbones. His dark blue vested suit was impeccable, matched by a white shirt, blue and red tie and handkerchief. There were those who had taken him for a dandy, to their regret.

"Thank you. There are a few there that are very rare," Crawton said, moving from the door to the wagon bar, where he poured himself a straight shot of twenty-five-year-old Scotch.

"Well?" said Eastham.

"Hopper will not be easy to deal with when this is all over," he said. *"They* will have to deal with us."

Crawton moved closer to the fireplace. *They,* of course, meant anyone who was not part of the organization.

"But as of this moment," Gibbs continued, "we have a more pressing situation confronting us."

Eastham began nervously to pace around the room. "Yes, Jesus Christ . . . the submarine surfacing . . . all those witnesses . . . what are we going to do? This whole thing could fall apart!"

"I don't think there's any danger of that," Crawton answered calmly. "We have Hopper and the evidence no longer exists. The witnesses are being seen to. Captain Richard has been given a story that should hold him just long enough for our purposes, and, besides, there's not a thing he can do without the photographs and transcripts."

"Then I take it all records of their being sent from Roosevelt Roads and received by the message center in the Pentagon have been altered or destroyed?" Gibbs asked.

"Absolutely! There is nothing," Crawton said. "Hays took care of that on this end and Tunner on the other. We even had dummy messages sent to Captain Richard from Admiral Tunner through Captain Gray, so Richard would be lulled into thinking another officer knew about the unidentified submarine."

"But can't Richard call an alert himself?" Eastham asked.

"Yes, but he won't." Crawton returned to the wagon bar and poured himself more Scotch. "For three very good reasons," he said. "First, he's been fed a message from his chief telling him to let Hopper take care of it. That should stall him for a while. Second, Richard knows putting the forces on alert costs millions of dollars, and the government does *not* look kindly on such an action without very solid documentary cause. Third, he did not have the opportunity to confer with Hopper. The Navy has a very firm chain of command, and the more serious the situation, the more important that chain of command becomes. You can be sure if Richard had gotten to Hopper, Hopper would have been at the CNO and there would have been some action taken, but he'll be quite reluctant to do anything on his own. And there is a fourth reason, now that I think about it: the submarine was sighted in international waters. Richard must have been aware of that fact and it probably caused him to hesitate. The longer he hesitates the more time we have to act. No, Captain Richard is not a threat."

"I told you your people had nothing to worry about," Eastham beamed to Gibbs.

Gibbs did not reply. Crawton sensed Gibbs was waiting for him to say something more, but he decided to wait him out.

"We're in the business of worrying," Gibbs commented after a while. "It is a good part of what we do. True, most of it is for nothing, but when something does happen it usually puts us in a position for changing it. In this particular situation, we *are* worried, very worried, because we can't do anything to alter the basic situation. Yes, we can block things here, and I must admit your people and some of my own have done it very effectively—*but* we are still faced with the fact that we have a submarine out there for a very specific purpose and that purpose could have been completely blown. Frankly, Admiral, we are concerned that something else might cause the submarine to surface."

"Yes . . . just what the hell could have caused Eldon to do something as stupid as that?" Eastham asked, his good spirits gone again, his face blotched with red.

"There's no way to even make an intelligent guess," Crawton answered.

"We received his message," Gibbs said. "And told him to proceed."

"Yes, I thought as much."

"We also ordered him to maintain radio silence until completion of the mission."

Crawton set his empty glass down on a nearby table and looked at Gibbs. "Mr. Gibbs . . . don't underestimate the pressure on Captain Crawton . . . I am sure he had a valid reason for being on the surface."

"I am sure he did," Gibbs said. "But you must understand that whether it was *valid or not,* it put the entire mission in jeopardy and by doing that, put some of the Company's people in jeopardy, too."

"I know that," Crawton snapped.

"So I must tell you, Admiral, that should something else force him to surface again," Gibbs continued unruffled, "we will not only withdraw our support and our people from the operation but we will do everything within our considerable resources to destroy the submarine."

Crawton paled. His right hand trembled slightly.

"I'm sorry, Admiral," Gibbs said. "But we had not counted on having to deal with so many different individuals, so many variables. What attracted us to the scheme initially was its simplicity. Now, it has become very, very complicated, indeed. I realize our planning *allowed* for such an emergency—but allowing for it and having it are very, very different things. I trust you see my point."

Crawton was silent for a moment, then, almost choking, he cleared his throat. "Yes," he managed to say at last. "Yes, I see your point."

"You hit the Admiral very hard," Senator Eastham said, as he drove back with Gibbs to Washington. "He looked badly shaken."

Gibbs eased the car from the ramp onto the highway. "There's just too much at stake here not to lay everything on the line. I don't think we're going to have any more problems, but if something should happen—the Admiral *had* to know where the Company stood."

After a few moments, the Senator asked, "Do your people anticipate a Russian counterstrike?"

"A minimal one," Gibbs answered, slowing down on the slippery road. "We estimate no more than a few million casualties and most of those will probably be in the northwest . . . missiles fired from Siberian bases."

"And the Russians, what about them?"

"Perhaps thirty million casualties," Gibbs said. "All of the *Barracuda*'s missiles are independently targeted multiple warheads."

Eastham gave a low whistle.

"Our people are sure it will be all over in forty-eight to seventy-two hours," Gibbs told him. "Should it continue for another forty-eight hours, we will be forced to commit land troops to invade Russia."

They fell silent. Gibbs reached over and switched on the radio and the strains of country and western music filled the car. Gibbs's gloved fingers beat lightly against the steering wheel, keeping time to the rhythm of the music. "How much do you know about this Captain Richard?" he asked.

"Just that he's Hopper's deputy, a career man," Eastham said. "Why?"

"He worries me. He's the last one left who knows anything . . . Maybe it would have been better to take him and leave Hopper . . ." Gibbs shook his head. "We can be glad for one thing, anyway: the Navy's so tight-ass that Crawton's probably right about the alert. Even if he gets suspicious, it'll take Richard days to set anything going on his own—and by that time it'll be too late. Still"—he smiled— "a little bit of insurance doesn't hurt."

"What kind of insurance?"

"Nothing for you to worry about, Senator. Just let us take care of it." Gibbs's fingers beat time. "We have specially trained people . . ." The car sped along the rain-slick highway. After a moment, he said, "Would you like me to drop you off at your hotel?"

"Yes, if it's not too far out of your way. It's—"

"—the Shoreham," Gibbs said. "I know. I'm staying there myself."

"I didn't know that."

"Just for the next few days," Gibbs said, as he eased down an exit ramp.

The Admiral remained in his study after Senator Eastham and Mr. Gibbs had departed. The butler brought him a ham and swiss cheese sandwich and a bowl of split pea soup, but after a few mouthfuls, he put the sandwich down on the plate and left it and the soup untouched.

Sitting in front of the fire, Crawton watched the flames slowly eat at a large log. Gibbs's words had not been wasted on him. From the very beginning, nearly two years ago, when he had first broached his plan to people at the top of the Company, he had been told that should anything go wrong with the plan, they would not only withdraw their support, but do everything in their power to destroy the officers involved. And now things had gone, well, if not wrong . . . at least a little off-track.

He could not even begin to guess why his son had allowed the *Barracuda* to be caught running on the surface. Though he was aware of the qualities that made Eldon a superior officer, he was not blind to his son's shortcomings. For one thing, Eldon was a womanizer. Even on that trip to Rio to meet with the Company men, he had spent a few days with a woman, who, of all people, had turned out to be the wife of an officer stationed at Roosevelt Roads. Thank God the officer was no one Eldon ever knew. And he had had the good sense to use another name and wear civilian clothes. But *why* did he take these risks? And then there was the problem of his ego.

Crawton knew his son envisioned himself as a combination of Captain Nemo and Sir Francis Drake. Though some element of that combination could work favorably for any commanding officer, it could also be a problem, especially if it overrode a man's judgment . . .

"Nothing," he said aloud, "should have caused him to surface." With a shake of his head, he stood up and went toward the bar cart. He poured himself another straight Scotch and was just about to drink it when the phone rang.

"Admiral Crawton here."

"Captain Morris, sir."

"Yes?" Crawton glanced at his watch. It was fifteen minutes past two.

"I was playing poker with some friends," Morris said. "Captain Paul Edwards has been having a very difficult time of it ever since the loss of the *Barracuda.*"

"More difficult than usual?"

"Yes . . . I think it is very close to the critical stage."

"How did the subject come up?" Crawton asked.

"Well, sir," Morris said, "one of the other players, Lieutenant Commander Jay Stewart, happened to mention in passing that he'd been in Rio recently . . . and he said he'd seen a man he could have sworn was Captain Crawton's twin."

"What?"

"After that, Edwards went to pieces."

Crawton forced his voice to sound casual. "Would you say that Stewart poses any threat?" he asked.

"No. It was just a comment."

"Did he ever meet Captain Crawton?"

"No, sir. He might have seen him at a reception, or perhaps remembered him from the photographs in the newspaper articles."

Morris repeated his conversation with Edwards and when he was finished, added, "He's working on intuition only, a 'gut feeling,' he said. But I don't like it. Edwards is smart enough to find something, if there's something to find."

"You mean in the transcripts of the court hearings?"

"Yes." Morris hesitated, then said, "He's already talking about the family connections between you and Senator Eastham. If he should want to investigate how the other officers aboard the Barracuda were chosen . . ."

"Yes," Crawton said, "I would have to agree that the Captain has come 'close to the critical stage.'"

"If I hadn't thought so," Morris said, "I wouldn't have called you at this time."

"Thank you, Captain . . . and goodnight."

"Goodnight, sir."

Crawton set the phone down. A tremor shook his body and he suddenly felt very cold. He looked toward the fire. It was still burning strongly. Then reached down for the Scotch and finished it in two swallows. He would call Gibbs in the morning about Edwards. No need to do it now. It was late, and he was tired, and from what Morris had told him, Edwards would probably just go home and sleep off his drunk anyway.

Crawton sat down again in the chair in front of the fireplace and thought back to the hearing. The truth of the matter was that he and the Senator had needed a scapegoat and Captain Edwards had been it. Between them, they had made it look to the press as if Edwards had personally sunk the *Barracuda,* either because he had designed faulty equipment or from more sinister motives. In the end they were forced to withdraw their statements by the presiding officer —but the damage had been done.

He would call Gibbs in the morning. Crawton leaned back, closed his eyes and soon began to snore loudly.

X

Richard brought Hilary back to his apartment, and without much further preliminary, they had found themselves in the bedroom. Their lovemaking had been deliciously passionate. At the moment of her climax, Hilary had pressed herself fiercely against him, and in a low voice repeated his name over and over again until with a last quick gasp, she had lain back sighing and contented. Asleep now, she lay nestled in the crook of Richard's right arm, her breathing slow and regular.

Until a few moments ago, Richard had been asleep too, but the sudden intrusion of a dream had brought him wide awake. Now the contents of the dream was slipping away, though, leaving in its wake only a vague feeling of apprehension.

Richard glanced at the green numbers of the digital clock on the night table. It was four-thirty. He watched several seconds flick by, then moved his eyes to the ceiling, feeling the warmth and pleasure of Hilary's naked body next to his. He moved his hand over her breast. From deep in her sleep Hilary made a low, throaty sound of contentment that made Richard smile. The circumstances of their meeting had been anything but auspicious, and he was not so naïve as to make long-range plans from one, albeit highly satisfactory, sexual encounter . . . but it was going very well, very well indeed.

Richard caressed her breast again and began to drift slowly back to sleep . . . when, unbidden, the photographs of the *Barracuda,* as he had spread them out on the floor of his office, came back to him. Damn. He opened his eyes, wide awake now. All right: Cob, Healy and Monte all knew something about the submarine. Cob was dead—but the other two men were available. One of them had actually seen the sub and the other had received the radio report. No matter how much Hopper knew about the situation, he would certainly want to question the man who had spotted the submarine. *Some* sort of an investigation would have to be made as to whether it was one of ours or one of theirs. . . . Richard was annoyed with himself. What was he the deputy for if not to get the ball rolling on this sort of thing?

He pulled himself up and reached across to the phone

on the other side of the digital clock.

Hilary awoke. "Nathan?" she said groggily. "What's . . . what's wrong?"

"Nothing, Hilary. I'm sorry. Please go back to sleep. There's just something I need to check out."

"At four-thirty in the *morning?*"

"Yes . . . please, go back to sleep." She yawned and drew the quilt over her bare breasts.

A few minutes later he was connected to the OD at Roosevelt Roads. Richard identified himself and said, "I want Lieutenant James Healy flown to Washington first thing in the morning. You contact Admiral Tunner and tell him I called and asked for the lieutenant. If the Admiral should want to confirm my request, he'll be able to reach me at my office."

"Is that name Lieutenant James Healy, sir?" the OD said.

"Yes. I don't have his serial number but—"

"Sir, we've had Lieutenant James Healy brought into the base hospital earlier. It may not be the same officer . . . but he was dead when he arrived."

"*Dead?*"

"Yes, sir. The police are reasonably sure he was the victim of a mugging. His wallet was found nearby, nothing but an ID card in it."

"Thank you," Richard said, stunned.

"Would you want to speak to Admiral Tunner?" the OD asked.

"I'll call him later in the morning," Richard replied, "thank you," and put the phone down. He realized he was sweating.

"What's wrong?" Hilary said.

Richard shook his head. Even if he knew, he couldn't tell her.

"Something to do with the Navy?"

"Yes," he answered. "But . . . let it go at that . . . I don't really know if anything is wrong."

"Nathan . . . just what *do* you do?" she asked.

"I'm deputy to the Chief of Naval Intelligence . . . a Navy spook, you might say . . . now please, no more questions."

He reached over and switched off the light.

Hilary moved close to him. Pressing her breasts against him, she said, "I can make you forget whatever is bothering you, at least for a little while."

Richard turned to her.

She reached down and stroked his penis. He kissed her hard, sliding his tongue over hers. His hands moved over the nipples of her breasts, teasing them into hard points. He was just about to kiss them when . . . he thought about CPO Monte. He drew away from her and again turned on the light.

"What are you doing now?" she demanded.

"I have to make this call."

She said, angrily, "You might at least have waited."

"I might have waited too long already," and a few minutes later he was again speaking to the OD at Roosevelt Roads. "I want the home address of Chief Petty Officer Dominic Monte. He's on leave."

"If you'll wait a few minutes, I'll check the roster."

"I'll wait." He sat, rubbing his eyes, and looked at Hilary.

She had left the bed and was beginning to dress. "You needn't bother about seeing me home," she said. "It's obvious you have more important matters to occupy yourself."

The OD came back on and gave him Monte's address and phone number. Richard scribbled the information down on a pad and then, to make sure he had it right, repeated it.

"Right, sir," the OD said. "Is there anything else?"

"No, and thank you again." Richard pressed the button to break the connection, waited for the dial tone, and immediately began to dial Monte's home number.

He looked up again. Hilary was wearing a sheer white bra and white panties. Her nipples were erect and the dark, triangular shape of her pubic hair showed clearly through the flimsy material. A sudden surge of heat moved through his groin.

"Just stay a few more minutes," he said to her, covering the mouthpiece of the phone with his hand. "I'm not doing this to upset you, or prove my importance. It's just that something—"

"Yes," a man answered on the other end.

"Is Dominic Monte there?" Richard asked, aware of noise on the other end that sounded like screaming or crying.

There was a moment of silence.

"Hello," Richard said. "Is anyone there?" Then, to Hilary, "I hope the hell I haven't been cut off."

"Who is this?" Another man's voice was on the line, a voice gruff and full of authority.

This time Richard was sure he heard the sound of women crying in the background.

"I said who is this?"

"Captain Nathan Richard, U. S. Navy. Who is this?"

"Detective Lieutenant Fioredeliso, New York City Police Department . . . Captain Richard, Dominic Monte was killed by a hit-and-run driver earlier this evening."

Killed. Richard shook his head and cleared his throat. "Lieutenant, I want you and your people to do *everything* possible to get some sort of a lead on the car. It's very urgent. I'm sorry I can't explain more now, but I will call you later in the morning. And, Lieutenant, under no circumstances is anyone to know that I called."

"I'm not sure I understand."

"I'm not surprised," Richard answered. "At this point I'm not sure I do either. But I think I can tell you, Lieutenant, that unless coincidences come in threes, CPO Monte was *not* a victim of a hit-and-run driver."

"Sir?"

"I'm sorry, I really can't say any more now. We'll talk later." He asked the Lieutenant for his phone number and thanked him for his cooperation. When he put the phone down, he turned to Hilary. She was completely dressed now and adjusting the jacket of her pants suit. "If I asked you to stay, to wait for me, would you?"

"Where are you going?"

"Back to my office," he answered, slipping on his shorts.

She hesitated, walked to the window, then turned to face him. "I'll go back to my place . . . If you still want to, call me later in the afternoon."

Richard crossed the room to where she stood, put his arms around her and kissed her long and hard. "It was good," he said, "very good."

"For me too," she whispered.

They kissed again and held each other for a moment. Then, moving away, he continued to dress.

November 17th. Ship time: 0630. I made the usual morning inspection of the boat today. Some of the crew looked at me questioningly, or at least I thought they did. I will have to watch for further signs of any sort of disquietude among them. I spent several extra minutes talking to a few of them about their duties aboard the *Barracuda.*

I also spent time with Lieutenant Commander Howell. He was his usual self. Of all of my officers, he is the most serious. The responsibility for the missile launch will be his and he looks upon the task with the same intense fierce sense of duty that must have possessed the saints and martyrs of an earlier time.

For that matter, I think that is the attitude of all the officers aboard. There *is* something holy about our mission, something, if I may say so, as sacred as the wresting of the Holy Land from the Saracens.

My Exec, Tad Haywood, put it rather well two nights ago, when we were discussing the future. He said, "When the time comes for us to talk about this mission to our children and grandchildren, how will we ever be able to explain how we felt? How could we tell them that we did what we did because of the real love of our country, and our God, that we all share?"

None of us in the wardroom could answer him. Yet I am sure all of us have thought about the same thing many, many times.

If this experience has taught me anything, it has taught me to understand the essential reason why men like myself and my officers must take the lead over all others. We do know what the truth is; we are *not* moral relativists. God, this country has had enough of *them.* Our opposition is awash in confusion. To them, there are no absolutes. They exist in a world of grays.

A long time ago, my father taught me that there

is one God and that He sacrificed His only beloved Son for the salvation of mankind. Therefore, it follows that anyone who does not believe on the Lord, Jesus Christ, must be evil. As this holds true with individuals, it also holds true with nations.

This does not mean that I consider myself a saint. On the contrary, if I am anything, I hope I am a soldier of God and of my country. I am certainly not pure in heart. I know my own carnality and I am not ashamed of it. Women find me attractive. I have always taken this as a sign that I have been given a gift, in some mysterious way made a more potent man by the maker of all men.

When I was a child, father used to tell me there were certain men who were given special talents by the Almighty so that they might lead others. I soon realized he was talking, among others, about himself.

It's important to note the state of our country at the present time, since it played no small part in goading my father and those who rallied to this cause into action. We are a nation who, having won the greatest war in history, allowed our enemies to become strong and our friends to wither.

Our people are misguided by the press, by television and by writers who have given them the false illusion that races and peoples are equal, that the government should restrict the profits of those who employ hundreds of thousands of people, who create our prosperity.

We have given too much away to our own people, making them soft; and to foreign people, making them greedy and envious of us. We have bowed down to a handful of Arabs because they happened to have oil. We have bowed down instead of going to the Middle East and *taking* the oil for ourselves.

We have had a progression of weak and ineffectual presidents, with the exception of Richard Nixon, who would have done many great things, had he not been destroyed by a left-wing conspiracy. It is my genuine—devout—hope that once the machinery of government is in the hands of our people, Mr. Nixon or someone of his caliber will once more take an active role in the affairs of state. Of all our recent political figures, Nixon was the only one who not only understood, but worked hard to put the United States in its rightful position —here and overseas.

I am being summoned to the bridge.

End of entry, Captain Crawton, commander of the submarine *Barracuda*.

Hilary lived in a garden apartment. From her window, she watched Richard walk down the snow-covered path to his car, his high collar turned up, his white cap pulled low over his face. He turned and waved. She waved back.

A few moments later, Richard swung the car into the roadway and was out of sight.

Hilary lowered the shade and pulled the drawstring curtain closed, then unbuttoned her jacket and draped it over the back of the chair.

Her apartment was furnished in Danish modern, jammed with bookshelves filled mostly by art books and histories. In addition, several oversized art books sat on a free form table in front of an ecru tweedy couch.

She went into the bedroom, undressed, slipped into a light blue robe and, picking up the phone, dialed the Shoreham Hotel.

"Room 1628," she told the operator.

The phone rang twice.

"Gibbs," the man answered.

"It went well," Hilary said, leaning back on the pillow.

"I assumed as much. You would have called earlier if it hadn't," Gibbs replied.

"But not as well as you might think," she said.

"You did—"

"Yes, I did what I was supposed to do," she said, cutting him short. "But he's on his way to his office."

"Now?"

"That's what I just told you . . . He made several phone calls. One to Roosevelt Roads to check on a Lieutenant Healy and another to the home of a CPO Dominic Monte. He knows they're both dead," she said. "He also mentioned someone named Cob."

"What the hell were *you* doing while he was so busy on the phone?"

"I'm not even going to answer that . . . He's going to phone me later in the afternoon."

"Stay with him," Gibbs told her. "Maybe if you stay close enough, he'll live to have the memory of a beautiful love affair."

Hilary ignored the remark. She had worked for Gibbs for two years, and she knew what he thought of her. She was only his tool, to use for his own pleasure when it suited him, for the pleasure of others when he needed something. More often than not, it was information. Sometimes it was to be photographed in bed with a particular man. Gibbs used her in any way the situation demanded.

"What kind of a man is Richard?" Gibbs asked.

"In or out of bed?"

"Don't be a wiseass. I'm not interested in how well he fucks."

"He's good," she went on. "He's gentle, considerate and—"

There was an abrupt click on the line.

Hilary smiled and put the phone down. Within moments, it rang. "We must have been cut off," she said innocently.

"What kind of a man is he?"

Hilary hesitated. She had been about to say, *he's a better man than you'll ever be,* but the edge in Gibbs's voice changed her mind. "He's smart," she said. "I think he'll cause you trouble."

"Then *you* see that he doesn't. Show him some new wrinkles," Gibbs remarked acidly.

Hilary didn't answer.

"Look, Hilary, there's a great deal at stake here," Gibbs said more moderately. "We've got only two choices now: take Richard out, or keep him so off balance he won't be able to do anything until it's too late. I'll have to consult with the others about the first; as for the second . . . no matter what happens with this particular operation, we'll want to keep Richard under *close* surveillance. You understand me?"

"I understand you, but I don't know how long it'll work . . . He looks like the marrying kind to me," she said almost wistfully.

"Then marry him!"

Hilary pulled the phone away from her face and looked at it quizzically. Moving it close again, she said, "You drunk or something?"

"I'm perfectly serious. This operation is too important. If it fails now, we may try to launch it, or something similar to it, in a year or two, or maybe five. If we leave Richard alive—and we'll have to do some hard thinking about that

—he can only become more important in the Navy, and we'll have the inside track on everything he does. By that time you might even have a couple of kids . . . Listen, you marry and he will be your assignment. You'll never have to go to bed with another man, unless you choose to. Everything will remain the same, including your salary and you will continue to report to me, or someone like me."

"I'll think about it," she said.

"I know a number of women who'd get down on their hands and knees and thank me a dozen different ways for the opportunity."

"I said, I'll think about it," she snapped.

"When he calls," Gibbs continued, unruffled, "make an appointment to meet him at some restaurant for dinner. Then call me and tell me where you'll be. If I'm not here, leave the message with the room clerk."

"Why—"

"I might want to have a look at him for myself," Gibbs said. "After all, I already have something in common with the man."

"You miserable bastard."

Gibbs smiled and hung up.

Hilary slammed the phone down, leaped out of bed and started to pace back and forth. Gibbs never let her forget she had once been foolish enough to think that he had loved her.

The phone started to ring.

She glared at it and let it ring.

After the fifth time, it stopped.

Hilary smiled with satisfaction, turned and was about to go into the shower when the phone started again. Knowing Gibbs would keep at it until she answered, Hilary snatched up the phone and was about to tell him to *fuck off,* when she heard Richard say, "I tried phoning you from an all-night diner, but the line was busy."

"Oh . . . Nathan . . . were you just trying to get me? I thought I heard the phone, but I was in the shower." Weak, girl, weak, she thought to herself.

"It was me," Richard said. He seemed to buy the excuse.

"Where are you now?"

"In the mall of the Pentagon . . . Listen," he told her, "I really didn't want to leave you."

"If I didn't believe that," she said, "I wouldn't have asked you to call me later . . . You will call?"

"Yes." He laughed. "That's why I'm calling now—to tell you that I'll call later in the afternoon."

"Now that's really beyond the call—"

"No," he said. "I just wanted you to know—"

"Tell me when you see me."

"Will I see you?"

"That's why you're going to call, isn't it?"

"Yes," Richard answered. "That's why."

They said goodbye and, nodding with satisfaction, Hilary put the phone down. She slipped her robe off and stood naked in front of the mirror mounted on the closet door. Her body was still young and supple, she noted with satisfaction. She cupped her breasts and the memory of how Richard's hands had felt on them floated pleasantly through her mind. Her thoughts were becoming dangerously unprofessional, she noticed . . . and somehow she didn't mind . . .

Which was even more dangerous.

XI

Friday, November 17th
0630

Richard left the telephone booth and walked down the long corridor to the escalator. Despite his immediate concern over the deaths of the three men, his brief conversation with Hilary had filled him with a deep satisfaction. It had been a long, long time since a woman had touched him so strongly. There was something ineffably feminine about her, something that made him want to reach out and touch her hair, or the side of her face.

As he passed a men's room, Richard decided to stop and splash cold water over his face. Another officer was already there, leaning against the wall. The man's back was to him, but he could see the reflection of the man's face in the mirror above the wash basins. For a moment Richard said nothing, but then he realized the man was oblivious to his presence, had probably never even heard him come in. His face was filled with an expression of unbelievable pain.

Richard had heard from other officers about how badly Captain Edwards was reacting to the aftermath of the hearings on the sinking of the *Barracuda,* but this was the first time he'd actually seen him since the court of inquiry. Hopper himself had commented on it to Richard, not once but twice.

The first time had been shortly after the court had warned Admiral Crawton about making allegations against any officer without supportive evidence. Crawton had apologized, but insisted on adding, "If I am allowing my emotions to outrun my reason, it is only because my son was and still is the skipper of the Barracuda . . ." About a week later Hopper had remarked he had heard Edwards was drinking heavily. Not long after that, the Admiral mentioned that Captain Morris had been assigned by Research and Development to keep watch over Edwards's projects. "His drinking has become much worse," Hopper had said. "And there's some concern about the work he's been doing . . ."

Richard had worked with Edwards a few years ago on a project, and had found him to be a sharp, capable, intelligent man. He hated to see what had happened to him. And the *Barracuda*—maybe there was a question or two he could answer. Placing his hand on Edwards's arm, he said,

"Come on, let's go to my office and talk." Even as he spoke to him, he realized the man was crying.

"I can't take much more . . . I just can't—"

"We'll talk about it," Richard told him.

Edwards removed his glasses and wiped his eyes with a piece of paper toweling. Blinking and shaking his head, he said, "I'm not drunk . . . I was drunk. But I'm not drunk now."

Richard nodded. "That's all right. No need to explain. I just came in here to throw some cold water on my own face."

Edwards finally focused on who was talking to him and seemed slightly surprised. "It's Richard, isn't it? Nathan Richard? I haven't seen you since—"

"Since the inquiry. I know. Now why don't we go into my office. You'll be much more comfortable there than here."

Edwards seemed to lack the energy to resist. He nodded. "Finding me here must seem weird—peculiar as hell," he said in a low voice.

"It's not every day I'm found stumbling around at six-thirty in the morning in the Pentagon myself," Richard replied. He went to the sink, washed his face with cold water and, after drying it with a paper towel, led the way out of the men's room. His earlier expansiveness had vanished entirely. Edwards's presence reminded him that he had a job to do.

The two men went up to the fourth floor by escalator, neither of them speaking. The people on night duty were still there. Richard paused in front of his office to unlock the door and, reaching around to the left, switched on the light.

"Just drop your coat anywhere," he said, "and sit down."
He put his own coat and hat in the small closet near the
door. "Too bad we can't send out for some hot coffee," he
added, going up to his desk and scanning it for the Admiral's note.

"I'm not drunk," Edwards insisted.

"I could use the coffee myself," he answered, unable to
find Hopper's note. The more he looked, the more upset he
became—and the more doubtful that a man in Edwards's
shape could help him.

"Look," Edwards told him, "I think I'd better go home.
My wife will be worried . . . I was home . . . but I couldn't
settle down so I came here."

"I thought I'd left something on my desk," Richard muttered. "But I obviously didn't." He dropped into the chair
behind the desk. "Now tell me what the hell you were doing
here."

Edwards laced his fingers, leaned forward slightly and
looked down at the floor. In a nearly inaudible voice, he
said, "I came here to read the proceedings of the inquiry."
Then, looking up at Richard, "I know it's crazy, but I
thought I'd find something that would prove I wasn't responsible for the sinking of the *Barracuda.*"

"The results of the inquiry never said you were," Richard
replied, aware that Edwards's hands were trembling.

"Not in so many words," Edwards said haltingly. "But
—but I know what the feelings of the court were . . . I know
what they were."

No, Edwards wouldn't be any kind of help tonight. In
fact, he'd probably be better off with a psychiatrist. Still,
he'd invited the man up here . . .

"You came here to read the proceedings," Richard said.

"You woke up, dressed and came down here?"

"No," Edwards answered. "I was at my weekly poker game." He named all of the officers who were there. "I don't know exactly how the conversation got started. I did have a lot to drink . . . but I'm *not* drunk now."

"I can see that," Richard assured him.

Edwards looked down at the floor again, his fingers still tightly laced. "Mary, my wife, and I had had an argument . . . Things haven't been going too well between us since the hearing. But it's not her fault, it's mine." He glanced toward the desk.

Richard nodded. The man was obviously going to spill his guts out right there and then and there was nothing he could do to stop him. He could tell him to go or try to call a doctor, but either act would probably destroy Edwards even further.

He was casting around for a solution when Edwards said, "I had a few drinks. Then I heard Stewart say that he had seen someone in Rio ten days ago who looked exactly like Captain Crawton . . . someone, Stewart said, who could have been Crawton's double . . ." Edwards didn't notice Richard's sudden interest, and went on . . . "He said Crawton's double was with a woman, and from there, I guess, things got pretty bad for me . . . I spent some time with Morris after the game talking about the inquiry, then I went home . . . but I couldn't sleep . . . I kept thinking about the *Barracuda* and the inquiry, so I came here—"

"Did you find anything?" Richard broke in, trying to keep his voice steady.

Edwards shook his head. "Nothing. I left the reading room and went into the men's room . . . I must have been there quite a while before you came in."

Richard rubbed his chin, a hard knot forming in his stomach. He looked at Edwards. The man was definitely close to a breakdown, but maybe . . . ?

"I know what you're thinking," Edwards said. "And maybe I am a bit crazy—but something is all wrong about this business. I *know* something is wrong, but I can't put my goddamn *finger* on it."

"Stay there," Richard said, coming to a decision. Leaving his chair, he went to the wall safe. "I have something to show you." He made several turns of the dial in one direction and then in another. In a moment the safe was open, he reached in . . . the packet of photographs and tapes was gone. In its place was an envelope addressed to him. He went back to the desk and slit the envelope with a letter opener, and an instant later was looking at the Admiral's writing. It slanted to the left, he noted.

> Captain Richard—
> Situation under control. Needed our photos and tapes. I'll be gone for a few days.
>
> Hopper

Richard picked up the envelope.

That was Hopper's writing too . . . but it slanted to the right. It didn't make any sense. Was Hopper angry when he wrote the note and not angry when he addressed the envelope? A phone call might have come in between . . .

"You look disturbed," Edwards said.

"I am." Richard sat down, scanning the note again.

"I know this may sound silly coming from me, but if I can help . . ."

Richard took a few moments to fill and light his pipe.

From the handwriting on the note, there was no doubt the Admiral was angry—but there was no indication of anger in the *tone* of the note. It was almost casual . . . and then it struck him. Hopper had used the possessive pronoun *our,* but Richard had not had the time to mention anything at all to him about the photos and transcriptions of the tapes. Even if he had found out about them from a different source, he should have used *your* instead of *our.* Hopper was too much of a stickler for details to make that sort of error.

"I think I'd better go," Edwards said, standing up. "You look as if you already have enough to cope with . . . You don't need a psycho officer on your hands."

"Sit down!" Richard said sharply.

Edwards looked at him. "I don't think—"

"Captain Edwards, *I* don't think you're psycho," Richard told him. "Upset, yes, very upset—but you offered me your help and I'm going to take you up on it. Now, I want you to listen to everything I tell you and I want you to tell *no one* a word about it . . . Please, sit down."

Questioningly, Edwards took his place.

"Suppose I tell you that early yesterday morning a submarine was sighted in the South Atlantic that resembled the *Barracuda.*"

Edwards was on his feet.

"Sit down, goddamn it!"

"But—"

"Wait till I've finished." Richard continued his account of the events of the past twenty-four hours.

Edwards listened intently. He remembered hearing something about a freighter going down with all hands somewhere in the South Atlantic, but he hadn't thought much about it. And now he was being told that because of it, an RF4 had spotted a submarine resembling the *Barracuda.*

"As soon as the sub was spotted, Healy contacted his base," Richard went on. "We now have three men who were involved in the immediate sighting: the pilot, the operations officer and the base radio man . . . Later Cob and Admiral Tunner also became involved." Suddenly, Richard realized that of the first three men, only Riggs was alive. He stopped and wrote the name on his pad, under the names of the freighter and the Marine major who had been killed in the plane crash.

"Now, see if you can follow me," he said. "Cob is killed in a plane crash on the way to Washington to brief me—"

"Was that the incident you squelched?" Edwards asked.

"Where did you hear that?"

"At the poker game. I don't remember who said it, but your name was mentioned, and so was the Admiral's."

Richard made another note on the pad. "*I* didn't squelch it, and as far as I know, the Admiral didn't even *know* about the crash—and if he did, he wouldn't have had any reason to black out the incident."

"Sorry, Captain, but that's what I heard," Edwards said quietly.

Richard paused for a moment, nodded and then continued. "All right . . . Cob was dead. Then there was a phone conversation between me and Tunner. Tunner told me he would hold Healy on tap in case I needed him—but the radio operator had been given two weeks leave and Riggs was dispatched to the carrier *Saratoga.* In the meantime, I received the radio photos and transcripts of the taped conversations between Healy and Monte, the radio operator."

"Then you saw the photos of the sub?"

"Yes."

"*Well...?* Is it the *Barracuda?*" Edwards asked, moving forward.

"It could be . . . It could also be one of theirs modified to look like the *Barracuda,*" Richard answered.

"By why would they do something like that?"

"Good question . . . but listen to the rest of what happened first. I called Admiral Hopper to discuss the situation with him, but he had already left the office, and when I called him at home the line was busy." Richard blew a puff of smoke. "Now follow me very carefully."

Edwards nodded.

"Cob was dead . . . I continued to try to contact the Admiral, but the line was busy. Eventually I spoke to the Admiral's wife. She told me that he had had to go out of town for a few days and that he had left a note for me in the office."

"That was what you were looking for when we came in?"

"Yes—I never thought of going to the safe. Remember, Hopper didn't know about the photos."

"He could have found out."

"I don't think so . . . Anyway, about two hours ago, I suddenly realized I should have Healy flown up here and debriefed. I called Roosevelt Roads and I was told he had been stabbed to death, a victim of a 'mugging'—I know exactly what you're thinking. I immediately called Monte's home in Brooklyn—and he was dead, too, a 'hit-and-run accident' this time."

Edwards was on his feet now, pacing back and forth.

"Are you trying to tell me that Russian agents did all that?"

"I want *you* to tell *me,*" Richard answered. "Maybe we'll tell each other and come up with some reasonable explanation for it all." He gestured Edwards back to the chair and waited until he was seated before he said, "When I went to the safe, I found this note from Hopper." He handed Edwards the sheet of paper.

Edwards read the note and looked at Richard. "He obviously does know about the sub."

Richard shook his head. "I don't think so."

"But he says the situation is under control."

"The Admiral has a little habit. When he gets angry, he writes with his left hand. Not too many people know about that . . . Look at the writing."

"It slants to the left."

"Right. Now look at the word *our* . . . Hopper wouldn't make that mistake. He would use the right pronoun."

"I don't understand what you're trying to get at."

"Look at the envelope."

"The writing slants the other way."

"Something must have happened between the time he wrote on the envelope and the time he wrote the note."

Edwards shrugged. "I still don't see what—"

"What I'm trying to get at is that the *tone* of the note doesn't show any anger. When Hopper is annoyed with something or someone, he never has any qualms about showing it—but the language in that note isn't angry at all. And look at this: the word *our.* I hadn't even told Hopper about the material. He's a very meticulous man, he would never have said that. He would have said *your.*"

Edwards considered all that in silence, and after several moments said, "Maybe he was in a hurry, and just slipped.

And maybe he simply moved quickly from one mood to another. Until you see him, you'll have no way of knowing—"

"All right," Richard said. "Let's forget about the writing. Let's look at what we have. What we have are three men who are dead and an admiral who has suddenly left for an undisclosed destination with a packet of photos and transcripts that are directly related to an unidentified submarine—the same submarine that the three dead men knew about."

"Admiral Tunner knew about it and he's not dead," Edwards said.

"But can the three deaths be just coincidence?"

Edwards shrugged. "I suppose they could . . ."

"There's a fourth man, too, who as far as I know hasn't been killed . . . and that's the OPSO, Riggs. I'm going to pull him back to the States as quickly as possible. We've *got* to find out what's going on."

"But, tell me, Captain, granted all this is so . . . why would the Russians pick the design of the *Barracuda* to duplicate—and then take so much trouble hushing it up?"

"You tell me."

"I can't."

The two men became silent. Richard puffed hard on his pipe. He wondered if he had told Edwards too much. He went to the window; the day had begun, the sky gray with clouds.

Suddenly Edwards spoke, his voice very low. "Someone at the poker game, I don't remember who, said they had seen Admiral Hopper."

Richard turned from the window.

"Yes . . . I remember he said the Admiral was with

Crawton and another man, a civilian." Edwards looked at Richard. "He said Hopper looked angrier than hell."

Richard walked slowly back to the desk and sat down. After a moment, he looked up at Edwards. "I'm almost ready to begin wishing it *was* a Russian submarine. At least we'd know how to deal with it . . ."

Edwards went back to his chair. "What are you going to do?"

"Whatever I do, whatever *we* do . . . it must be with the utmost caution."

"Goddamn!" Edwards said, almost to himself. "Goddamn!"

A half hour later, Richard decided he had it, or most of it. There were still some pieces missing but . . . he knew there were some officers in the Navy, and in the other branches, who would like nothing better than to go to war with Russia, but he could never have conceived of any group taking matters into their own hands. Yet that was exactly what he was sure had happened.

"And Crawton tried to make the members of the court think I was a Russian agent," Edwards said bitterly. "How the hell could he do something like that?"

"How could he do any of what he seems to have done?" Richard said. "How could any of them do it?"

Edwards shrugged again and lapsed into silence.

"We've got to get all the facts," Richard said. "We've got to get them and put them before Admiral Powell, Director of Naval Security, every last detail. Otherwise, he'll think we're lunatics."

"Suppose," Edwards said, "he's part of it."

"Then we're dead." Richard was silent for a moment.

"While you're here, I'm going to phone Crawton—I want to find out what his reaction will be."

"To what?"

"I'm going to tell him I'd like to see him as soon as possible about an urgent matter."

"You'll be tipping your hand."

"No, I'll leave it vague. He can't possibly know how much I've learned in the last few hours. I just want to see how his voice sounds, see if it knocks him off balance a little."

"And if he comes, then what?"

"I don't think he *will* come. But if he does, I'll give him a story about wanting to retain him as a consultant, but the report not arriving yet, so I'll have to talk to him later. Or, better yet, *Hopper* will talk to him later . . . It's time we began to unnerve him a little. . . ."

"You know, I wonder how Senator Eastham fits into all this? Remember, he's related through marriage to Crawton —and at the Senate subcommittee hearings he made all that to-do about having two relatives aboard the *Barracuda.*"

"I forgot that Hayward was related to the Crawtons," Richard said.

"I'll never forget any of it," Edwards said bitterly.

Richard said nothing. Edwards had good reasons for bitterness, but he hoped his feelings wouldn't interfere with what they had to do.

"Don't worry," Edwards assured him, almost as if reading his thoughts. "As much as I can, I'll keep my personal feelings out of this."

Richard gave an appreciative nod and flipped the cards on his Rolodex until he came to Crawton's. He was about to lift the phone when it began to ring. He glanced at

Edwards and picked it up. "Captain Richard here."

"You sound so official." Hilary laughed.

The sound of her voice sent a ripple of pleasure through him, and he turned slightly away from Edwards before saying, "I'm involved in some official work."

"I just wanted to tell you something," she said, "and then I'll go away."

"I'm listening."

"You sound anxious to get rid of me," she teased.

"No . . . but—"

"Is someone with you?"

"Yes."

"Who?"

"A friend of mine."

"Will he be a friend of mine as well?"

"I hope so."

"What's his name?"

Richard laughed and said, "Captain Edwards." Hell, he shouldn't have . . . well, it couldn't do any harm . . . "Now please tell me why you called."

"I just had the feeling that you would like to know how good it was for me," she said in her throaty voice. "And that I wish you were with me now."

Richard flushed. Her frankness excited him. "Thanks," he answered. "Thanks."

She said goodbye and hung up.

Richard faced Edwards and put the phone down. He needed a moment or two to regroup.

"I didn't think you'd be the type to blush," Edwards remarked with a smile.

"Neither did I—at least not at my age," Richard answered. He was still annoyed at himself for letting Edwards's name slip out. Hilary would be all right, but he'd have to watch himself. Picking up the phone again, he punched out Crawton's number.

After four rings, a man came on who announced he was the butler.

"This is Captain Richard of Naval Intelligence. I would like to speak to Admiral Crawton."

Silence, then a flurry of voices in the background. A moment later, the butler said, "The Admiral is not available."

"Please have him phone me when he can—it's very important."

"I'm sorry, sir, but he will be away for several days. May I take a message?"

"No," Richard answered. "No, thank you, but please have him get in touch with me when he calls in." He put the phone down. "Admiral Crawton is 'away' for several days," he told Edwards. "But I'm sure he was there." He glanced at his watch. Eight o'clock. In another hour, the day shift would be in. "Well, at least Crawton's wondering why I called so early in the morning. Now"—he reached for his pipe—"I want the names of all the officers at your poker game."

Edwards took the pad from the desk.

"Next to each name, put down where they can be located during the day." Richard lifted the phone and put through a call to Roosevelt Roads. In a few minutes he was talking to the officer in charge of travel arrangements and found out that Lieutenant Commander Riggs had been issued a three-day pass en route to his assignment to the *Saratoga*.

"What airline did he fly?"

"TWA out of JFK in New York," the officer said.

Richard thanked him, cut the connection and immediately put through a call to TWA in New York. It took him a while, but he finally discovered that Riggs had flown to Milan the previous night and had been booked by the airline into the Hotel la Scala.

When he finished, he showed the information to Edwards. "Should I order him back immediately or handle it another way?"

Edwards stood up and stretched. "The sooner he's in our hands, the better. We can't risk another 'accident.' "

"You're right. I'll have orders waiting for him when he reaches Gaeta. That should get him back to Washington in a matter of hours."

"What do you want me to do?" Edwards asked.

"Come back here about 1200. I should have several things cleared up by then. I'll want you with me when I go to Admiral Powell."

Edwards gathered up his coat and hat. "A few hours ago," he said, "I was ready to pack it in . . ."

Richard stood up and walked around to the front of the desk. "There's no need for explanations," he said. "No need at all." He put his arm around Edwards's shoulder. "not too many men would have been able to hang in the way you have. It took a great deal of courage to do that."

"No," Edwards said. "If I had courage, I would have fought back months ago, when all this started . . . I would have found a way of clearing myself of any suspicion."

"But you couldn't have. You would have had to know what we know now—and even now we're guessing at a great deal—"

"Do you think Admiral Powell will make the same guesses?"

"Captain, by the time we see Powell, we'd better not have guesses anymore. We'd better have facts." Richard walked Edwards to the door, shook his hand and watched while he strode down the corridor, a man delivered of demons. Then he turned and walked quickly back to his desk, to wrestle with his own.

That morning Gibbs looked like any other tourist whose reverence for Lincoln had brought him out early in the chill gray to the massive monument that commemorated the man. Despite a strong north wind that blew the newly fallen snow into the open ends of the monument, several other visitors were already there.

Gibbs stayed against one wall, his breath steaming in the cold air. He was worried. Richard! Gibbs was convinced now the organization had made a mistake in not killing him as soon as he knew about the submarine. Hilary could have done it last night—no mess, no fuss. But he was too conspicuous, the organization said. Cob, Healy, Monte, that was one thing, but with Hopper gone, they couldn't risk eliminating his deputy, too. Besides, Richard couldn't possibly put all the pieces together in time . . . Gibbs snorted in disgust. And now Richard was holed up in the Pentagon. It was hell to get at someone in there. Well, if he couldn't kill him, he could shut him up in other ways . . .

Sensing someone coming, Gibbs turned and saw Crawton. He went toward him and the two men moved off to the other side of the monument.

"What do you know about Edwards—Captain Edwards?" Gibbs said, without greeting.

Crawton remembered Morris's call the previous evening. "Well, I—"

"He was with Captain Richard early this morning," Gibbs said.

Crawton did not ask him how he knew. He accepted what he was told as a fact. "I received a call from Morris late last night about him," he said. "I was planning to tell you this morning . . . Morris thought he was becoming critical."

"I think so, too."

"Is that why you asked me to meet you here?"

"No." Gibbs looked hard at Crawton. "I want to know more about Captain Richard. What kind of a man is he?"

"I don't understand your question. If you're asking whether he's a good officer, the answer is, yes, he's a good officer . . . but you're asking something else—"

"How far will he follow something?"

"All the way, I'm afraid."

Gibbs nodded and pulled his tan camel's hair coat more tightly around him. "Do you think he might be convinced to see things our way?"

"Not a chance," Crawton said. "He hasn't got the . . . perspective we have. Richard phoned me early this morning, by the way. He was told that I would be out of town for the next few days."

"It might have been wiser to speak with him," Gibbs said, taking a cigarette out of the gold case. "By now he has Hopper's note and knows his photos and transcripts are gone. He might have asked you to help him." Gibbs lit the cigarette with a gold lighter. "Richard has become more of a problem than we thought he would. He might have to be taken out."

"Oh, but surely that isn't necessary," Crawton said. "With Hopper gone, it'd be much too obvious. You'd have

Navy Intelligence swarming all over the place and who knows what they might find. And besides with all his evidence gone, there's nothing he can do, I told you, to get anything going in the chain of command before it's too late, and—"

"Save your breath, Admiral, I've heard it all before. I've got some other plans for Richard right now—but I'm telling *you* right now, if anything more happens with him, my people want him *dead,* and I assure you, he is going to *be* dead."

Crawton agreed shakily.

"I've taken another small precaution, by the way," Gibbs said. "Part precaution, part warning. You can add Richard's nigger woman to the list."

"His secretary?"

Gibbs nodded. "She signed for the package of photos and transcripts of the tapes. We couldn't have her telling anyone about them. And I think Richard will get the message."

"Is she *dead*—"

"No . . . worked over so it'll be a while before she can tell anyone anything. And to make it look better, raped— I'm told she has a stunning body."

Crawton started to walk away.

"Listen, Admiral," Gibbs said, moving in front of him. "It wasn't *my* son who put that sub on the surface. It was yours—and it was *your* boy who waltzed around Rio with a woman who happened to be the wife of another *naval* officer."

"I don't think we have anything more to say to each other."

"No, Admiral, not for the moment but just you get off your high horse," Gibbs said, stabbing his gloved forefinger at Crawton's chest. "Now you go out to that hunting lodge and stay there until I call for you."

Crawton started to object.

"Don't say anything, Admiral," Gibbs told him in a low voice. "This whole operation is being held together by spit and luck and a few dead men, so just don't say anything." He turned and walked hurriedly out of the Memorial, down the steps and across the mall . . . Men like Crawton angered him. They wanted the damn world and were willing to kill millions to get it. But when it came to knowing the details about killing one man or beating up on one woman, they turned pale and got sick to their stomachs. They'd rather not know about the dirty work . . .

Hopper came to complete wakefulness with the suddenness of a man forcing himself out of a bad dream. He blinked several times and rubbed his eyes, momentarily disoriented, but then the memories of last night came flooding back. Warily, he looked about.

He was in one of the bedrooms on the upper floor of the hunting lodge, a small room sparsely but comfortably furnished. Downstairs, he could hear sounds, dishes clanging, the mutter of voices—there seemed to be several of them. The pungent smell of coffee and bacon floated up the stairs, making his stomach growl, and reminding him that he had had nothing to eat since lunchtime yesterday. He had refused all food last night—a silly gesture, he realized, but one which had made him feel good. Turning to the window, he found himself looking out at a picture postcard winter scene, all snow and trees. At least five to six inches had fallen during the night. In the gray light of the overcast morning, he could see past the nearby copse of birches to where the woods really began.

Hopper rubbed his stubbly chin. He had never cared for Crawton, or his son. They both had ability but what they couldn't achieve by honest means, they used political influence to obtain, or money to buy. There had always been something weasely about Crawton, despite all his righteousness—and now it was obvious from his comments last night that he was actually involved in a plot of some kind to take over the government. Hopper had no idea how it was supposed to work, but it was plain the Navy was somehow involved, otherwise why bother to kidnap him?

The sound of an approaching car drew his attention and he walked to the door and listened. The car stopped. The downstairs door opened. Hopper could feel the sudden surge of cold air gusting through the narrow space beneath the bottom of the door.

Noises of snow being stomped off boots, and a voice: "It's colder than a witch's tit outside."

"Close the damn door!"

The door slammed shut.

"The wind's blowing the damn snow all over the place," the first voice said. "Can hardly see where you're going sometimes."

The sound of footsteps faded and the voices became muffled.

Hopper went back to the window, aware now that the wind had mounted; as he watched, intermittent gusts sent flurries of snow swirling to his left. He sat down on the bed again and looked at his watch. It was 8:30. With any luck, Richard would find the note in about half an hour. He counted on his deputy to be smart enough to realize that something was wrong and to alert Admiral Powell. They'd certainly worked long enough together for Richard to spot the clues in the note . . .

But what if Powell didn't believe him? There was no solid evidence, after all, that he had been kidnapped, just that he'd gone on a trip. And what if Richard didn't go to his safe today, or for several days? It depended upon whether Richard realized the value of whatever was in the package . . . what *was* in that damn package? It was obviously important enough to prevent Richard from having it.

He began to pace. Crawton's action puzzled him: It was plainly one of desperation. He couldn't hope to get away with it unless—Hopper stopped. Unless the time schedule was so short there wouldn't be time to search for him. Unless Crawton expected to be running the government very, very soon.

He sat down again and organized his thoughts. If Crawton's plan worked, there would no longer be a place for Hopper in the Navy. Sooner or later, he would be killed or some pretext found for imprisoning him. And should Crawton's gamble fail . . . There was no chance he would be allowed to walk away. Crawton surely knew he would go straight to the President.

"Either way," Hopper told himself aloud, "I'm dead."

He rubbed his chin, stood up and walked back to the window. The snow was marked with the footprints of birds and he saw several sparrows resting in the birches. He had always enjoyed watching birds and though he had never really gotten serious about it, he and Peggy always had enjoyed walking through the woods, paging through their field guides, seeing what they could identify. He wondered if he would ever—

Footsteps on the stairs brought him around to face the door, and in a moment the decision was made. Reaching down into the empty fireplace, he picked up one of the andirons. He would have only one chance.

The footsteps came closer.

Hopper moved to one side of the door and lifted the andiron.

A key clicked in the lock. "Admiral?" The door swung open and the man stepped into the room. "Admi—?"

Hopper brought the andiron across the side of the man's head, dropping him to the floor, blood springing from the wound.

The man groaned.

Hopper struck him again, this time breaking through the bone of the skull. He bent over the dead body and removed the .357 magnum from the man's shoulder holster. A few minutes later, he was out of the room and quietly making his way downstairs.

He hoped he could get his hands on one of the M-16s the guards carried. He could do a lot of damage with that before they stopped him.

Just as he reached the bottom step, one of the guards came out of the kitchen. Hopper shot him in the head.

XII

Friday, November 17th. Ship time: 0830. Another incident. I was summoned early this morning to the bridge because our sonar had picked up another submarine, moving west on a bearing of 190 degrees. I am not certain whether it was one of ours or a Russian sub. When first picked up, it was doing about twenty knots, then it slowed to six. I kept the *Barracuda* directly in the interface between two temperature differentials.

The crew stood at battle stations for almost two hours, and there seemed to be an enormous amount of tension. I noticed that one of my junior officers, Lieutenant Carson, had developed a twitch under his right eye.

The sub altered its course several times in what appeared to be a search operation, but it could not find us. I did not change our heading for fear we would lose the protection of the thermal interface.

After sonar contact with the sub was finally lost and we secured from battle stations, I held a short discussion with the officers in the wardroom about the morale of the men. Most of them were of the opinion I should make some sort of an announcement to the crew regarding the nature of our mission without actually revealing anything specific. Some of the crew already harbor suspicions that we are not on an ordinary mission, I was told, and the rest are simply uneasy. I could tell that for myself. Regardless of the opinions of my officers, however, I will say nothing more to the crew.

Certainly it would be easier for me to tell the men the exact nature of our mission and therefore let them share the burden of carrying it to successful completion with me. But that burden is meant only for me and my officers. The decision to launch the missiles will be mine. In the past, men like Caesar, Alfred the Great and Napoleon have led whole armies against their enemies, but I have less than two hundred men against one of the most powerful nations in the world. It is a heavy responsibility.

The less the crew knows about the real nature of our mission, the more secure the success of the mission is. Though I am proud of their technical performance, I cannot trust them. Despite our care, I cannot be sure that a Russian agent or sympathizer is not among their number. I cannot risk having one or more of them misunderstand what we are being sent to do.

End of entry, Captain Crawton, Commander of the submarine *Barracuda*.

One by one, the members of the day staff drifted into the office of Naval Intelligence. Richard told several of his junior officers to pass the word that Admiral Hopper would not be in for the next two or three days, but did not say why. This was for no one else's ears yet.

About ten after nine, he became aware of his secretary's absence and had one of the other Waves call Donna at home.

"There's no answer, sir," she reported. "Do you want me to keep trying?"

Richard shook his head. Strange, Donna was always punctual. He went to the file on Donna's desk where she kept the carbon copies of all the receipts from message center. The receipt for the package from Roosevelt Roads wasn't there. Crawton didn't miss a trick, Richard thought grimly.

Assigning another girl to his desk until Donna got in, he went to the washroom to shave and freshen up for the day ahead—he was feeling all right considering how little sleep he'd had, but Richard wondered how long he could hold up. On his way back, he stopped at the message center and chatted for a moment with the lieutenant on duty.

"By the way," Richard said, "I seemed to have mislaid one of my file receipts for a package that was sent up to me from Roosevelt Roads yesterday. Would you mind checking your own file and giving me the receipt number for my files?"

The lieutenant nodded obligingly. Going to the computer console, he typed out the previous day's date, the point of origin and the recipient. "It'll be up on the screen in a couple of seconds," he said with a smile.

Richard couldn't see the computer display screen but he could see the lieutenant's face. A moment later the smile changed to a frown. He looked up. "Sir, nothing was sent to you yesterday from Roosevelt Roads. Are you sure it was yesterday?"

"Absolutely sure. Could the information have been incorrectly entered on the computer tape?"

"Might have been," the lieutenant conceded. "Doubt it, though. I'll run a scan of the past five days, if you want me to, but it'll take me an hour or two, depending upon the amount of traffic here."

"If you would," Richard said. "Oh, one more thing . . . did Captain Gray receive a message from Admiral Tunner yesterday?"

The lieutenant's fingers flashed quickly over the keys. Moments later, he looked up and shook his head. "Sorry again, sir. But if either of the messages are important, I'm sure we can pick them up from the message center at Roosevelt Roads."

"Were you on duty here yesterday?" Richard asked, clearing his throat.

"Yes, sir. I went off at four-thirty," the young officer answered, his voice betraying some anxiety now.

"Lieutenant, I want you in my office sometime during the next ten minutes," Richard told him. "You are not to tell anyone where you're going. Is that clear?"

"Yes, sir."

Richard turned and hurried back to his office, the lieutenant looking after him with a clearly worried expression. As he walked through his doorway he sensed immediately that something was wrong. Several of the Waves were clustered around Donna's desk and a few of the officers were gathered in a group near the door.

Commander Don Smith, a large man with a ruddy face, separated himself from the other officers. He glanced toward the Waves and bobbed his head in Richard's direction. The women drifted apart.

"Sir," Smith said, "I just took a call from the Washington police . . . I think we'd better go into your office."

Richard led the way and went to his desk.

Smith closed the door. "I'm afraid that Donna was found—"

Instantly, Richard was on his feet. All this time, he hadn't thought about Donna's safety at all. She'd had no idea what the package contained, but she could certainly verify its arrival. If she was dead—

"She was beaten and raped," Smith said in a low, grim voice. "The police theorize two, possibly three, hoods broke into her apartment and worked her over. They took some cash and the usual stuff they could fence . . . These goddamn punks—"

"Will she live?" Richard asked.

Smith nodded. "But she's in pretty bad shape. Her jaw is broken . . . she won't be able to talk for a while."

Richard sat down, his thoughts full of anger. And something else, too. Fear.

Riggs, Edwards and himself were the only ones left outside the cabal who knew anything about the submarine.

"I took the liberty of having her moved from the city hospital to Bethesda," Smith said.

"Thank you," he replied, only half-listening.

"One of the lousy punks even had the gall to phone the police and tell them to go to the apartment."

Richard carefully picked up his pipe and began to fill it with tobacco. He forced himself to remain absolutely calm. She was alive, that was something at least. He wanted to run and comfort her—but now they had no more time to lose. He lit his pipe and, motioning with it to Smith, said, "Commander, what I am about to say is going to sound unusual. For the next day or two, I am going to need your full cooperation. I want you to do exactly what I tell you without telling anyone—and I mean *anyone*, in this office or any other—what you are doing."

Smith nodded, puzzled.

"Sit down," Richard said, pointing to the chair next to the desk. "Commander, I need two other officers in this section who you would trust with your life. And I mean exactly that—your *life.* "

Smith shifted his weight uneasily from left to right. "Well, sir," he said after a moment's thought, "I would choose Lieutenant Frank Holmes and Lieutenant Commander Thomas Carey, I guess."

Richard flicked the switch on the intercom and told the girl substituting for Donna to have Holmes and Carey come to his office immediately. Then he added, "I'm expecting Lieutenant Rawson. Have him wait. And hold all calls, *unless* it's the Admiral." He turned the intercom off and sat back, waiting. The smoke from his pipe rose in a thin column toward the ceiling. From his desk he could see the sky through the window. The clouds were still very gray.

A soft knock sounded at the door and the two officers entered the room.

140

"Sit down, gentlemen," Richard said.

Holmes was a young man with copper colored hair, blue eyes and a heavy dose of freckles. Carey was darker complexioned, with strong features and coal-black eyes. Both had been fighter pilots. Richard knew them, if not well—they were good men.

"What I'm going to say," Richard cautioned them, "is in the realm of top secret. Nothing, repeat *nothing,* is to go beyond this room. Each of you will be assigned a seemingly unrelated task, but I can assure you that they are not unrelated and that they have a distinct connection to what has just happened to my secretary. Regardless of what the police say, I can assure you that she was not the victim of a robbery. These were no ordinary hoods."

The three men waited for Richard to explain more, but he said, "That's all I can tell you now." He put his pipe down and looked at Smith. "Commander, here's what I want you to do, and please, no questions. "I want a roster of all the officers on the *Barracuda.* I want to know how they were assigned to her. Then I want their personnel files. I don't care how you get them—but I want them here by 1200."

"Yes, sir."

"Holmes, I want you to do exactly the same thing for the officers of the *Bluefin.* "

"Do you want any additional information on the officers?" Holmes asked.

"Only what I asked for," Richard said. Turning to Carey, he gave him the list of men who had been at the poker game with Captain Edwards. "Run a check on them through NIS. If anyone asks questions, tell him we're compiling a list of officers who might be eligible to serve . . . to serve as our Naval attaché in Peking once we establish formal diplomatic relations with China."

"Yes, sir."

The Wave in the anteroom came on the intercom. "Sir, I am sorry to interrupt, but there's a detective on the line from the New York City Police. He insists on speaking with you."

"I'll take it," Richard answered and picked up the phone. "You must have read my thoughts, Lieutenant. I was going to call you as soon as I finished my meeting here."

"You were right, Captain," Fioredeliso said. "Monte was not the victim of an ordinary hit-and-run driver. I had some of my men check the people on the street: one old man saw a car parked near a hydrant. There were two men in it *and* he saw the car pull away and head for Monte . . . Now get this, about two hours ago a stolen car turned up in the Sixty-third Precinct with blood splattered on its hood—the blood type matches Monte's."

"Are you sure?"

"Absolutely."

"Now what will you do?"

"Well, Captain, a couple of goons must have been paid for the job. We'll put feelers out to see who suddenly turned up with more bread than he had a few days ago."

"If you get them," Richard said, "I want a crack at them before anyone else, and I mean anyone else."

"I'll do my best," Fioredeliso answered.

"Keep them out of the station house, Lieutenant—what's the expression? Keep them on ice—that's it, keep them on ice until I can come up to question them or have some of my men do it."

"That serious?"

"Much more, Lieutenant. Believe me."

The two men exchanged a few more words and Richard put the phone down. "A CPO was killed in New York last night," he said to the officers in front of him. "I can tell you this much: that killing and what happened to my secretary are connected." He ignored their look of surprise. "It's almost 1000, gentlemen," he reported, looking at his watch. "I want all of you back here by 1200."

As the three officers stood up to leave, he motioned Smith to remain seated. He waited until the door closed before he asked, "How well are you wired into the Marine Corps? I mean, could you have someone do a quick trace for me?"

"Yes, I think I could—but I wouldn't be able to have it by 1200."

Richard picked up the phone and put through a call to the travel order section at Roosevelt Roads. A short time later, he was speaking to the officer in charge. "Yes. This is Captain Nathan Richard, Naval Intelligence. I would like the serial number of a Marine Major Paul Sanders. He was one of the two passengers who were killed in the plane crash yesterday." Richard cupped his hand over the mouthpiece and said to Smith, "If I was a betting man, I'd lay odds that he can't find it."

"But a copy of a travel order is usually kept on file—"

Richard waved him silent and removed his hand from the mouthpiece. "You have it! Excellent. Wait until I have a pen . . . go ahead . . . number 0–327–785 . . . Well, thank you very much. Now, listen carefully, I want the copy sent to my attention—and mark it *top secret.*"

He put the phone down and gave the slip of paper with the number on it to Smith. "Check it out," he said. "Tell me everything there is to know about him."

"I'll do my best, sir," Smith answered as he stood up.

"If I didn't think that was true," Richard said, "I wouldn't have given you anything to do." He stood up, too, and walked to the door with Smith. When he opened it, Lieutenant Rawson was there, sitting in one of the chairs. The young man was very pale. Richard shook Smith's hand and wished him luck, then, without saying a word, motioned to Rawson with his finger and disappeared back inside. By the time Rawson entered the room, he was seated back behind his desk. As Rawson stood there, he deliberately emptied his pipe, filled and lit it, then sat there a moment before turning his full attention to the lieutenant. He regarded him silently for a few seconds, then spoke. "Was there any possibility of someone erasing the data from the tape while you were there?"

"No, sir."

"Then what happened to the data, Lieutenant?" Richard said in a hard voice.

"I . . . I don't know, sir."

"Did anything unusual happen yesterday?"

"Not that I know of, sir."

Suddenly Richard was out of his chair. "Something *must* have happened, Lieutenant. Think!"

"W . . . well, last night there was ten minutes of down time to remove a snag in the tape. But that's not—"

Richard snapped up. "What time?"

"The log book says 1900," Rawson answered.

"Who authorized the repair work?"

"I don't know, sir."

"Isn't his signature in the log?"

"It should be, but I didn't see it . . . Whoever it was probably forgot to sign it."

Richard nodded sharply and sat down. "Thank you, Lieutenant. You've been very helpful and I apologize for coming down on you so heavily. You may go back to your duty now—but, Lieutenant . . . if anyone should ask where you were, you tell them you had a case of the runs. You understand me?"

"Yes, sir," Rawson answered, not understanding much at all. But he was more than glad to get out of that office.

Richard was alone again. He walked to the window and looked out at the snow-covered ground and beyond it to the slate-gray river in the distance. It was a gloomy landscape, but not nearly as gloomy as the landscape in his brain. He shook his head and walked back to his desk . . . He had set the wheels in motion. He could do nothing more now but wait—and that was the most difficult thing of all to do. . . .

XIII

They met in a small luncheonette on O Street, two blocks away from the campus of Georgetown University. Gibbs arrived first and chose a booth for two in the back. He sat, waiting, ignoring the dozen different odors in the air, the ripped red plastic of the booth. The large plate glass window at the front dripped with condensed moisture.

A waitress came to the table and asked for his order. He told her that he was waiting for someone to join him, and she made a comment about it being almost lunchtime. Gibbs looked up at her, his eyes narrowing. The woman started to say something, changed her mind and with a shrug, walked away.

Gibbs lit a cigarette and turned his attention to the large glass window. Everything on the other side of it was runny, like an impressionistic chiaroscuro gone wrong. Hilary had taught him about that. But his interest in the window had nothing to do with art. In some unknown way, it evoked the past for him, the small, ugly candy store his parents had owned in the East New York section of Brooklyn. All his life he had carried parts of that squalid store around with him. At this particular moment it was the window and probably the heavy smell of food. His mother had cooked in the store . . . Various other times, he'd remembered the large dark wood and glass candy cases, the white marble top of the counter, the tables and chairs made of wood and heavy metal wire . . .

Gibbs realized he was looking at Hilary. She was standing at the door, looking for him, dressed in a blue trench coat and yellow wide-brimmed hat. He waited, and after a few moments she saw him and came over. She removed her hat and coat silently, revealing blue jeans and a heavy, dark red sweater. The jeans hugged her body tightly, while the loose sweater showed only a hint of breast. That was just like Hilary, Gibbs thought. Couldn't decide whether she was a good little girl or a whore.

She sat down, still without a word. She was annoyed and the expression on her face showed it. Despite the other odors, Gibbs was very much aware of her perfume, musky and deeply sensual. He stubbed out the rest of his cigarette and looked around for the waitress. Yawning, the woman came to the table.

"I'll have coffee," he said. "And what would you recommend?"

"Whatever you want, we got it. Everything is good," the woman answered.

"Everything is too much," Gibbs told her with a narrow smile. "I want one thing."

"Okay, the corned beef."

"Corned beef?" he asked, looking at Hilary.

"Just black coffee," she said.

"Corned beef on rye and coffee," Gibbs told the waitress. Lighting another cigarette, he watched her slouch away, and leaned forward. "The problem is becoming more of a problem, Hilary, and your friend is becoming more curious. Is there anything I should know?"

"I haven't spoken to him in hours."

He shook his head. "We're working in the dark. He must be on to something."

"I told you all I knew—"

The waitress came to the table and set down Gibbs's sandwich and Hilary's coffee. As soon as she was gone, Gibbs said, "I want you to see him tonight."

"You told me that this morning. You're repeating yourself."

Gibbs took a bit out of the sandwich and chewed it very slowly. After he swallowed, he said carefully, "Then I advise you to listen to me the first time. If you work at it, you *might* be able to keep him alive."

Hilary put the cup down and spoke in a low, intense voice. "We've been together too long, Gibbs. If he's not dead yet, there are other reasons for it. I know that, Gibbs, and you know I know."

Gibbs had no intention of answering. He took another bite out of the sandwich and chewed just as deliberately. "Call him later in the afternoon," he said. "I think I have something that might bring the two of you closer *much* faster."

She looked at him quizzically.

"Leave that to me," he said. "I should have done it sooner, but so many things had to be taken care of so quickly that I couldn't get it going until a few hours ago."

"What is it?"

"I'll let him tell you," he answered, wiping his lips with a paper napkin. "And if you're any good I'm sure he *will* tell you . . . Now if you'll excuse me, I have some phone calls to make."

Hilary nodded and drank the rest of her coffee.

Ten minutes later, Gibbs returned and started on his sandwich again. "What's the rest of your schedule this afternoon?" he asked.

"I'm going to the library."

"No," he said, "you're going with me and I'm going back to your place . . . At least for an hour or two."

"Like hell!" she said, starting to her feet.

His right hand grabbed hold of her wrist. "No matter what you say," he told her, "we're going back to your place. I've just got time for a little matinee."

Hilary sat down, shaking.

"That's better," he said, picking up what was left of his sandwich. "Don't worry about it. I promise you I'll never tell Richard I was the one who broke you in, or even that you once loved me . . . I don't think he would find it very romantic."

"I hate you," she said in a tight whisper. "I didn't think I could ever hate anyone, but I hate you, Gibbs."

"That should make the afternoon all the more interesting," he said, lifting the coffee cup to his lips.

Admiral Crawton sat in the right-hand corner of his chauffeur-driven limousine, his eyes closed. The coffee and toast he had had after his meeting with Gibbs were giving him severe heartburn now. Gibbs was proving to be a source of great irritation to him.

He had been warned about Gibbs by some of the other people in the Company and in Naval Security—the kind of man who always managed to take charge of things, they'd said, and that was exactly what Gibbs was doing. He was ordering all the moves. He had the manpower to do it.

There was no question the man was efficient. It was Gibbs who had masterminded the sale of the *Shark*, a World War II, Gato-class submarine, to the Chilean government, and arranged its modifications to look like the *Barracuda*, before sinking it in fifteen hundred fathoms of water. It was even Gibbs who had arranged to have enough atomic waste aboard so that the salvage crews, sent by the Navy to recover what they thought were pieces of the *Barracuda*, would get the appropriate readouts.

Still, Crawton was beginning to mistrust the man—and he decidedly did *not* appreciate the remarks Gibbs had made about his son. No matter what danger Gibbs had faced in his career with the Company, he could never know the emergencies the skipper of a submarine might have to face. Crawton only wished *he* knew what had caused Eldon to—He gave a deep sigh. Enough about that. No more than two days now until the *Barracuda* completed its mission. Once the government was under his control, he would deal with Gibbs. He'd withstand the man's insults until then, but when—

"Sir," the chauffeur said, "there's smoke up ahead . . . It looks like it's coming from around the lodge."

Crawton opened his eyes. It was true. In front of them, windblown black smoke smudged the gray sky.

"Step on it."

"I'm going as fast as I can, sir. The road's very slippery here."

Crawton frowned. The car swung around a curve and started up a steep incline, when suddenly he heard the staccato cough of an M-16.

"Good God, what the hell is going on up there?"

"Sounds like rifle fire, sir."

"Forget about the ice," Crawton barked. "Just step on it."

The vehicle leaped forward, but an instant later began to fishtail. The driver fought the wheel and barely brought the car under control. His voice strained, he said, "Can't do it, sir. The road is too icy."

Crawton didn't answer. All the scenarios for failure were flashing through his mind.

Two more shots rang out.

"Those sound like handguns," the chauffeur said.

Another short burst from an M-16 broke the stillness of the countryside.

"Those damn shots have an echo," Crawton raged. "Don't those idiots know that?"

The car moved up another hill and swung onto the snow-covered dirt roadway leading to the lodge. The going was even slower now, the snow holding them back, but finally they burst out of the woods and could see where the smoke was coming from. To the right of the house a car was burning.

"Stop!" Crawton ordered, and jumped out of the car. Simultaneously, a burst of fire erupted from the woods, just beyond the burning car. Two rounds whacked into the trees alongside Crawton and he dropped to the ground. Another round ripped through the left front tire, ricocheting off the inside rim of the right front tire.

The chauffeur opened the door and dived onto his stomach.

Crawton didn't have to be told what had happened. Somehow Hopper had managed to get his hands on an M-16.

There was more firing now, from the direction of the house.

"Try and get around him," Crawton yelled to the chauffeur.

There was a moment of silence as the chauffeur crawled to the woods. When he seemed to be safe enough, he leaped up—and a burst from Hopper's M-16 sent him flying backward. The man fell to the ground, his chest torn open.

Another fusillade erupted from the house. Under its cover, Crawton watched a man run out the front door and along the side of the house until he gained the woods.

The firing stopped. Except for the pounding of Crawton's own heart, an awful stillness fell upon the snow-covered landscape. The air smelled of burning rubber and gunpowder.

Crawton knew if he stood up, Hopper would not hesitate to cut him down.

Another burst of fire came from the house. The figure of a man darted through the trees, clearly trying to move around Hopper's right flank and come up behind him. Dimly, through the trees, Crawton could make out Hopper's crouching figure now.

Crawton cupped his hands and called out, *"Hopper* . . . Throw down your weapon . . . This is Admiral Crawton. I promise nothing will happen to you."

No answer.

Crawton could see the man moving up behind Hopper.

Several more shots from the house slammed into the woodpile in front of Hopper.

"Listen to me," Crawton shouted, hoping to divert him long enough to allow his man to get close enough. "Give me a chance to talk to you. There's a place for you with us . . . Hopper, believe me. Nothing—"

The man was suddenly a few yards in back of Hopper and must have made a noise, for Hopper whirled around, his finger squeezing the trigger, his rifle bucking. But the man was too quick. He dropped to the ground and snapped off two rounds from his .357.

Hopper fell back against the woodpile, sending a stack of kindling to the ground. His hands still clutched the M-16. He struggled to lift it.

Another round from the .357 tore the weapon from his grasp.

"He's had it," Crawton's man called, getting to his feet.

Crawton pulled himself up and ran to where Hopper lay, his right arm smashed below the shoulder, blood coming out of his stomach. Behind him, more men came running from the house.

"It did not have to be this way," Crawton said, kneeling down next to him.

"No . . . other way for me," Hopper gasped. "No other way . . . had to do as much . . . damage as I could." He began to cough. Blood.

"But you could have been one of us," Crawton said.

Hopper shook his head, he began to cough again, then suddenly struggled to sit up. "Charley . . . oh, Charley . . . I . . . I've missed you . . ." He fell back and his head slipped to one side.

"Who the hell is Charley?" asked the man who shot him.

"His son," Crawton answered, closing Hopper's eyes. He stood up and cleared the tightness in his throat before he asked, "How much damage did he do?"

"Killed two others besides your chauffeur," one man said. "Who'd have thought he still had it in him?"

"I should have," Crawton answered. "I knew him well enough . . . even riding a desk, he never gave an inch without a fight."

"He sure as hell did fight," the man agreed.

All that morning, Richard had tried to phone Hopper's wife, but always the line was busy or no one answered. Shortly before 1100, he contacted the Washington police and asked them to check the Admiral's house.

Ten minutes later he received word that no one was there. He made a note of the police officer's name and thanked him. Peggy Hopper, and perhaps her dinner guest too, had certainly been taken from the house by the same

154

group that had kidnapped Hopper, though he couldn't guess why they had waited so long.

At 1115 a Wave brought him a decoded communiqué from Atlantic Fleet Headquarters.

> To DNI—Wash via Lan Flt Hq.
> From—Atk Sub #47 Com Sub Lant
> Brief contact w/Goblin 0630 . . . Lat. 30° 15', Long. 19° . . .
> Searched area . . . Contact lost. Initial goblin head; ENE, Est. Sp. 45 knots.

Richard stuffed the communiqué in his pocket and hurried to the Operations Room. There, a large electronic map showed the position of every vessel in the United States Navy, as well as the position of every ship on every ocean of the world. The information was constantly being updated, a computer feeding in new entries, course calculations and recalculations.

Captain George Simione was the duty officer, a slender man with a brown handlebar moustache. He and Richard had been junior officers together aboard the submarine *Nautilus*.

"How are you on Russian subs?" Richard asked him.

"Which ocean?"

"North Pacific."

Simione called out instructions to one of the junior officers, who immediately relayed them to the petty officer. Within moments, several red flashing lights appeared on the status board. Three were grouped in an arc around Alaska, two others were north of Japan and five appeared off the coast of China.

Richard nodded his head appreciatively. "Pure magic."

"Do you want information about any particular one of them?"

"No, thank you. I just need a refresher on how some of this works for a project I've got coming up. Can you show me what we have in the South Atlantic?"

Simione relayed more instructions, and soon the red lights in the North Pacific disappeared, to be replaced by several green ones in the South Atlantic.

"Which one, say, is the *Sting Ray?*" Richard asked.

Simione motioned Richard to follow him to a computer terminal marked, FOR DUTY OFFICER ONLY. "What's her number?"

"Forty-seven."

The Captain typed out the submarine's identifying number. Immediately, instructions appeared in green on a display screen. Simione followed them in order, and as he typed the last letter of the last word, the screen went black.

"Watch the status board," Simione said.

All the green lights stopped flickering, except one. The *Sting Ray.*

"What's her patrol area?"

Simione fed another series of instructions into the computer.

An orange rectangle encompassing several thousand square miles of ocean suddenly enclosed the green flashing light. The *Sting Ray*'s purpose apparently was to guard the approaches to the Strait of Gibraltar, a mission probably shared by one of two other attack submarines.

"What about the Mediterranean?" Richard asked.

Within moments a dozen different green lights were flashing from one end of the Mediterranean to the other.

Richard nodded in satisfaction. "Thanks for the information," he said. "This should be a great help."

"Anytime," Simione said. The two men exchanged a few more remarks, mainly about the weather and how difficult it was to drive with snow on the ground, then Richard left the Operations Room and started back to his office. He liked Simione and hoped he wasn't involved with Crawton's group of officers.

"Someone has been trying to phone you," the girl in the anteroom told him. "But he wouldn't leave a number where he could be reached."

"Did he give his name?"

"No, sir. He said he'd call back in ten minutes or so. He should be calling soon."

Richard sat down at his desk and took out the communiqué received earlier. The goblin could have been a Russian submarine, but he was willing to bet that it was the *Barracuda.* He reached over for his pipe and was about to walk over to the map of the world that stretched over most of one whole wall when the girl came on the intercom. "That gentleman who has been calling you is on one, sir."

"Captain Richard."

"Back off, Captain," a voice said.

"What—who is this?"

"I said, back off, Captain. Don't follow through . . . we have your son, Captain, he's right here with us. I understand how fond of him you are . . . I'm sure you wouldn't want to see anything happen to him."

"Who *is* this?"

The line went dead. Richard put the phone down and using his handkerchief, wiped the sweat from his forehead. His hand was trembling. Oh, he knew who it was all right. The bastards, the incredible bastards . . . He leaned back into his chair and closed his eyes. He must not panic.

He leaned forward suddenly and placed a call to New York. Why, Nathan dear, how nice to talk to you . . . No, Henry wasn't home yet for lunch, he was a little late, but he should be in soon . . .

A call to Henry's school. Yes, Henry Richard was on the early lunch shift today, he'd left for home a little while ago . . . Why, was there something wrong?

No, no, nothing wrong. Richard closed his eyes again. They had pushed him into a corner. He didn't doubt for a moment that they would kill his son, if, as they said, he did not back off . . .

He stood up and began to pace. If it had been his own life . . . but his son . . . he had always felt that whatever he achieved in his lifetime, whatever rank he finally reached, would be strictly a personal accomplishment, but his son . . . Henry . . . came from both him *and* Joan. He was the best they'd both been able to give to the world . . .

Richard stopped at the window. It was still raining. But what kind of a world would it be if Crawton and his friends succeeded? "I can't back off," he said aloud. "I just can't let them get away with it." And maybe he wouldn't have to.

He walked quickly back to his desk, picked up the phone and put through another call to New York. "Lieutenant Fioredeliso. Captain Nathan Richard. What I'm about to say is going to sound very unusual, Lieutenant, but I think you know enough by now to realize that we are in a very unusual situation. I need your help, Lieutenant. My son has been kidnapped . . ."

For the first time in months, Captain Edwards felt like a human being again and not like a disembodied spirit. He drove slowly down the street, whistling a few bars from the Mendelssohn Scotch Symphony, barely noticing the gray skies or the snow that blanketed the streets. He'd gone home, had a few hours of sleep, and now he was wide awake. He knew that if Richard hadn't found him when he had, it would have been all over. He would either have returned home and blown his brains out, or simply prolonged the agony a few years by drinking himself to death.

From the way Mary had looked at him that morning, he was certain she had seen the change in him. But he'd been able to say nothing more than, "Things are going to be different. I promise you."

As usual, she had responded with her *I heard that one before* look.

He had not pushed his claim. In the past months, he had made too many promises he had never kept. But as he had left the house, he had suddenly reached for her and gathered her in his arms. "I love you, Mary . . . I love you."

Taken completely by surprise, she had pressed herself against him and for the first time in weeks, they'd met in a long, lingering kiss. "Don't you know," she whispered, "that I love you, too?" If he'd had more time, he would have taken her to bed then and there.

But he had to go back to the Pentagon to meet with Richard . . . and take the story of the *Barracuda* to Admiral Powell . . .

Edwards saw the green light on the corner of Monroe and 18th change to yellow, and slowed, anticipating the red. He glanced up into the rear view mirror. The car in back of him was slowing, too, and swinging to his left. Edwards looked ahead. The light had changed to red, and he came to a stop. A moment later the other car pulled alongside of him, and, glancing at it, he saw there were two men in it. The driver was Captain Morris.

Edwards touched his horn.

The man next to Morris turned to him and cranked down the window.

An instant later Edwards saw the muzzle of a revolver. Before he could press down on the accelerator, there was a pop. The glass window of his car shattered and the bullet entered the right side of his chest. A moment later, the second one smashed into the left side of his head. Edwards slumped over the wheel. He did not hear the horn blow, and blow and blow. . . .

Richard put the phone down, his hands trembling, his forehead still sweating. Henry . . . he'd done what he could. Fioredeliso had agreed to go out on a limb for him, was even now gathering men together through unofficial channels to hunt for his son. He seemed like a good man . . . For a moment, Richard had second thoughts about what he was doing, Henry's danger weighing heavily on him. But then he put them aside. Crawton's cabal and the mission of the *Barracuda,* whatever it was, put an even heavier burden on him. He could not let them get away with it. It was the kind of command decision every officer had to make at one time during his life. Except usually it involved his own life and the lives of the men who served under him. This time the life at stake was all he had left of his marriage—

The phone rang.

"Captain Richard here," he said, clearing his throat.

"This is Simione. I have something that might interest

you. Entirely slipped my mind when you were here. Curious thing, that number forty-seven of yours turned up a goblin submarine at Lat 30° 15′, Long 19° this morning. You might want to come see how we show it. Any goblin becomes a yellow flashing light. We get a few each day and they move around. More than half are our own. If they can be identified as ours or theirs, they become either a green or a red light."

"That *is* interesting," Richard said. "I think I'll stay put for the moment—but, George . . . I want you to hold that goblin in the data bank. If it's sighted again or identified, I want to be notified immediately."

"Something going on, Nathan?" Simione asked.

"Nothing I can talk about now, George, but I'll let you know if I can . . . By the way, if anyone should ask you why the goblin's in the bank, tell them it's part of special NATO exercises. And if someone *should* ask, I'd like to know who it is, *regardless* of his rank."

"Is that a formal request, Captain?"

"Yes," Richard answered. "And thanks for calling." He put the phone down and dug the communiqué out of his pocket, setting it down on his desk. No matter what additional information his subordinate officers brought in, he would have to go to Admiral Powell. He had so little on paper, but it was all in his *head,* dammit! Powell would *have* to see the connection.

He dialed Admiral Powell's number and got his deputy, Captain Philip Goree. Richard arranged to meet with the Admiral at 1500.

"If it could be sooner," he said, "I would appreciate it."

"I'm afraid not, Captain," Goree answered in a slow southern drawl. "The Admiral has a meeting at 1400 and an appointment for lunch. But if there's any change, I surely will call you."

"Thank you," Richard said. "I wouldn't press if the matter wasn't so urgent. *Please* see what you can do."

"I understand," Goree told him.

Richard put the phone down—no, I don't think you do understand, Captain Goree—and glanced at his watch. It was 1205. The men were late. He filled his pipe, lit it, and sat back to think for a moment. The slice of sky through the window at the other side of the room was still gray.

Suddenly Richard was overcome by an intense desire to speak to Hilary, to hear her low, laughing voice and sensuous purr. He knew it was crazy, but he was actually thinking of reaching for the phone, when the intercom came on and he was told that Commander Smith had arrived. Behind him were Holmes and Carey.

Richard greeted them and noted, "We should be joined by Captain Edwards. I'll give him a few more minutes before we begin."

They nodded and sat down.

Richard glanced at his watch again. It was 1210. He turned on the intercom and asked the Wave at the desk to phone Captain Edwards's home. "Find out what's keeping him, and what time he'll get here." Then, to the other men, he explained, "Edwards was here with me a good part of the night. He may be having some difficulty pulling himself together."

"Edwards," Smith repeated. "That name is familiar. Is it—"

"Yes, he's the man who was responsible for the design of the special—"

"Excuse me, Captain," the girl said over the intercom,

162

"but I think you had better pick up on one."

Richard reached for the phone. "This is Captain Richard," he said. "To whom am I speaking?"

"Officer Ferguson of the Washington police," the man answered.

A sudden chill gripped Richard.

"Captain Edwards is dead. He was shot to death a few minutes ago."

"My God . . . where?" Why the *hell* had he let Edwards go back home—

"About a mile from his home, at the intersection of Monroe Street and Eighteenth. We don't have too many details. I was sent here to bring his wife to the city morgue to make a positive identification."

Richard took down the officer's name and badge number and explained who he was. "Captain Edwards was due at a meeting in my office . . . If I can be any further help, please call me."

He put the phone down and in a low voice told the three officers seated in front of him what had happened.

"But why—" Lieutenant Holmes began.

"Because he was connected with the *Barracuda,*" Richard answered sharply. "That's right, gentlemen, the *Barracuda.* And I should have *known* it could happen. The same thing could very well happen to any one of you as soon as they—*whoever they are*—find out you are involved in this investigation. So we have no time to lose. I'll explain to you all later. We'll start with you, Commander Smith, tell me what you found."

Smith was obviously bursting with questions, but he put them aside. "Marine Corps Major Paul Sanders," he said. "No one by that name or rank, according to the personnel headquarters of the Marine Corps, has been assigned to Roosevelt Roads, at least not for the last ninety days, and —this is the clincher—his service number matches the number of a *Major Paul Sanders* who was killed in Nam during the 1968 Tet offensive."

"Are you absolutely certain?" Richard asked.

"Yes, sir."

"Go on."

"Then I checked our own Bureau of Personnel," Smith said, "on the question of the *Barracuda* officers. *Every officer* aboard the *Barracuda* was requested either by Captain Crawton or by some other senior officer aboard the submarine."

"That's very unusual, isn't it?" Richard commented.

"Yes, sir. Extremely. But that's not all. I was interested in *why* those particular officers were appointed, what special thing they had in common, and this is what I found: each of their families is *very* wealthy, I mean, millionaires —and every one of them contributed *big* to Senator Eastham's last campaign."

"Then what we have is a group of handpicked officers whose economic, and no doubt political, background is exactly alike."

"It appears so," Smith answered.

Holmes and Carey exchanged looks of surprise.

"Anything else?" Richard asked.

"No, sir."

"Tell me about the assignment of the officers to the *Bluefin,*" Richard said, turning to Lieutenant Holmes.

"Everything routine there, sir," Holmes replied. "Assignments made in the usual way. The only request was by the skipper for the engineering officer—they'd served together on two other submarines."

Richard looked at Lieutenant Commander Carey.

"Right," Carey began, and ran down the list of the men at the poker game. Halfway through, he stopped.

"Now, Captain Morris," he said, "is with Research and Development. He's got an excellent record, but look at this . . . on several previous occasions he has been TDY'd to the CIA where he's worked with a man named Robert Gibbs and another one named Harris, James Harris."

"Gibbs," Richard said. "Wasn't there someone by that name involved with the sale of the *Shark* to Chile?" He glanced at Commander Smith.

"Yes," Smith answered. "I have a file on him . . . but nothing that would connect him to the CIA."

"Of course not," Richard said. "Could you get the file, please?"

Smith left the room and a few minutes later returned with a 5" × 8" blue index card. He handed it to Richard, who began to read it aloud.

"Gibbs, Robert. Age thirty-seven. Occupation . . . Import-Export." Richard stopped. "That sure gives a man a great deal of latitude, now doesn't it?" He went back to the card. "Arranged for the sale of the *Shark,* a WW II, Gato-class submarine, to the government of Chile, in association with former Rear Admiral Crawton. A friend of Senator Eastham . . ."

He stopped and set the card down. "That's enough. Gentlemen, I'm sure I need not caution you again about the sensitivity of this matter. No one must hear what has just been said in this room. I want to thank you for your good work. Carey, I want you to go down to police headquarters now and find out what you can about Edwards's killing.

Holmes, follow through on the officers of the *Bluefin*. I want to divert attention from the *Barracuda*. Commander Smith, stay here a moment." He reached over to the intercom and told the Wave the time for the daily intelligence meeting had been moved up to 1300.

"Contact the necessary officers and extend my apologies for the inconvenience."

"Yes, sir."

He flicked off the intercom and turned to Smith. "Commander, please cover the daily briefing . . . If anyone asks where either the Admiral or myself is, tell them that Hopper is out of town and . . . I was detained by an unexpected situation. Think of something."

"I'll do my best," Smith answered.

Richard waited until the three men had left the room and gazed out the window at the gray November day. Cob . . . Monte . . . Donna . . . now Edwards. Who was next? Himself? . . . Henry? He put it out of his mind and began to organize the evidence for Admiral Powell.

> Friday, November 17th. Ship time: 1200. This afternoon my officers, especially Tad Haywood, my Exec, finally prevailed upon me to speak to the crew. Haywood told me many of the men were becoming more and more apprehensive about the nature of the "cruise," sure now that we were not on the usual mission.
>
> I used the PA system to tell them their real mission: that the men and officers of the *Barracuda* had been chosen to carry out a preemptive strike against Russia—this nation's, and the world's, foremost antagonist and premier international mass murderer for over half a century.
>
> I spoke to them much the same way King Henry

V spoke to his men before the great battle of Agincourt, if I may be so presumptive. I put it in simple terms. I told them the honor bestowed upon us would live throughout the future history of our country. I told them we were of one mind and one heart, that great care had been taken to provide us with security. And that was why, except for very brief radio contact with a secret radio station, we had maintained our radio silence for over three months.

For all practical purposes, I said, we on the *Barracuda* no longer existed. I did not go so far as to tell them the complete truth. I explained, for instance, that the Navy's own tender, *Subic Bay,* had been sent to accomplish certain rewiring needed for our particular mission. We rendezvoused with the *Subic Bay* two weeks before we were reported lost. The rewiring was done, however, by individuals who were not members of the Navy. I did not mention this fact to the crew. Nor did I mention that the *San Rafael,* the South American ship which supplied us with fresh food, was not doing so on the orders of the Navy.

I was sure several of the more intelligent men aboard would ask more questions. I knew that uppermost in their minds would be the question of whether or not we would survive the mission. I anticipated this by telling them that once we fired our missiles, we would immediately rejoin the Sixth Fleet.

But this is only part of the truth. My orders are to contact the Commander of the Sixth Fleet and, in the name of the Provisional Government which will be headed by my father, demand that he turn his command over to me. If his response is negative, then I am ordered to sail immediately for home.

I assured them that there was absolutely no chance of the Russians ever locating us. I said, "Our superior technology and seamanship will make it impossible for them to locate and track us." Then I closed by telling them, "We were given a great trust and I intend to do *everything* in my power to honor that sacred trust of my country and my God."

I would have thought my words would have inspired them, but it seems that has not happened.

Since then my officers tell me the men are more restless than ever. Many are congregating in small groups and talking among themselves in whispers that quickly fall away when an officer approaches. We are no longer a ship with a single entity. We are divided into officers and men.

Tad has already apologized to me for having insisted I share something of our purpose with the crew, but I told him I blamed only myself for having let him sway me from my own judgment.

I must expect a certain amount of discontent from the crew. Some of them will undoubtedly use the situation to be less than efficient in the performance of their duty. They will become malingerers, finding whatever excuse is at hand to avoid work. This cannot be permitted to happen. I have already issued orders that no member of the crew will be excused from his assigned watch unless they have their division officer's signature.

My chief concern is that we have no agitators aboard. Men with a verbal gift can easily lead others astray, and I have been told there are several that should be watched very closely during the next forty-eight hours. At the least suspicious move, I will have them arrested. But only temporarily.

After we make our strike, they and the rest of the

men should be only too happy to share in the honor that will follow. They will be proud to tell others that they were a member of the crew led by Captain Eldon Crawton. The men who complain most now will be the very ones who boast the most later. They will say that on such a day at such a time we struck a blow for the whole world's freedom.

Within a matter of a few hours we will be in the Mediterranean and another full twenty-four hours will put us in firing position.

End of entry . . . Captain Crawton, Commander of the submarine *Barracuda.*

XIV

Friday, November 17th
1500

"Goree said it was urgent." Admiral Louis Powell removed his horn-rimmed glasses and looked up from the papers on his desk.

"Yes, sir," Richard said.

Powell gestured him to a chair at the right of his desk. The Admiral was a bear of a man, red-faced, with bright blue eyes. During World War II, he had taken command of a destroyer when every other man on the bridge had been killed by fire from a Japanese cruiser and he himself had sustained two severe wounds, and single-handedly maintained the helm. His action had prevented the loss of the ship and a substantial part of its crew, and for it he was awarded the Navy Cross.

"Goree," Powell said, "you stand by. I might need you."

Captain Goree nodded and sat down to the Admiral's left. He was physically very different from Powell, tall and trim, handsome, with light brown hair and hazel-colored eyes. He had twice been shot down by the North Vietnamese while a carrier pilot in Vietnam. Once, he had bailed out over the jungle and made it back to the south after a trek of forty-five days. The second time he had landed in the South China Sea and had had to paddle around in a rubber raft for the better part of a week before being rescued by a search chopper.

Powell leaned back in his chair and pushed his glasses to one side. "Having to wear these whenever I want to read," he said, "is the one thing about getting old that I don't like." Then with a grin he added, "The other things haven't bothered me so that I'd notice them."

Richard smiled. So did Goree, even though he'd heard the line before. It was Powell's standard way of breaking the ice.

"All right," Powell said, "tell me what's so urgent?"

Richard took a deep breath. "Sir, in the past two days a series of events has occurred, events so extraordinary I have only been able to piece them all together myself a few hours ago. And, taken together, I believe they pose a critical threat to this country's security."

Powell's eyebrows shot up. "Why aren't you telling this to Hopper?"

"I'll explain that in a minute, sir." Richard opened a manila folder. "I've made some notes," he said, "of all the salient facts. But I will start by telling you that the *Barracuda* did *not* go down with all hands some three months ago. If my guess is correct, she is at this very moment somewhere off the Strait of Gibraltar."

Powell moved slowly forward. "I'm listening," he said.

"On the thirteenth, the freighter *African Wolf* sent a May Day from fifteen degrees north latitude, fifty-five degrees west longitude. She had sustained an explosion and was sinking rapidly. She went down with all hands."

Powell glanced toward his deputy.

"There was a memo on it," Goree said. "It was filed under disaster, cause unknown. No additional information came through."

"Are you going to tell me the *Barracuda* was responsible for the sinking of the *African Wolf?*"

"No," Richard replied. "However, on the sixteenth, an RF4 out of Roosevelt Roads, on a routine flight, spotted the wreckage of the *African Wolf,* went down for a closer look and to photograph it, and—"

"Goree, do we have anything about that sighting?" Powell asked.

"No, sir." .

Powell's eyes moved to Richard. "Any particular reason why your people didn't send through a memo?"

"The reason why there's no memo will become clear, Admiral," Richard said.

Powell nodded and told him to go on.

"Before spotting the wreckage, the pilot of the RF4 came on to a new heading of 014 degrees. He was just about to climb when he saw a submarine on the horizon. Immediately he reported the sighting back to the base, which taped the report. He made two passes over the submarine and photographed it."

"Then you have the tape transcript and the photographs?"

Richard shook his head. "No. I did *see* the photographs and scan the transcript, but I don't have them now. I'll explain that, too."

"Captain," Powell told him, "either you're leaving something out or you're not making sense. What does the *African Wolf* have to do with the submarine you say a pilot saw and photographed?"

"Looking for the *African Wolf* made it possible for Lieutenant Healy to see the submarine."

"Where is Lieutenant Healy?"

"He's dead, sir."

Powell raised his eyebrows again.

"The police said he was knifed to death by a mugger," Richard said. "But in the light of other events, I doubt that. I think he was murdered."

"You'd better go very slow, Captain . . . very slow," Powell cautioned him. He slipped on his glasses and began to make notes on his pad. "Continue."

"Initially, there were five people who knew about that sighting," Richard said. "Admiral Tunner, the base Commander; Lieutenant Commander Riggs, the Duty OPO; Lieutenant Commander Cob, the base Intelligence officer; Lieutenant Healy, the pilot; and Chief Petty Officer Dominic Monte. Of the five men, three have died, all in the space of about twenty-four hours. Healy was knifed by a mugger. Cob died in a plane crash—he was on his way here to see me. And CPO Monte was killed by a hit-and-run driver."

Powell turned to Goree. "Do we have anything on the deaths of those men?"

"Yes, on Lieutenant Healy and Commander Cob. Reports came through in the routine manner."

"Monte was killed in Brooklyn," Richard said. "I have been in touch with the police there and told them not to release any information unless they cleared through me first."

"Tunner and Riggs, where are they?"

"Riggs was TDY'd to the carrier *Saratoga* and Tunner is still at Roosevelt Roads. Sir, let me explain . . . I was in touch with Cob before he was killed. He wanted to protect the information until the submarine was positively identified. He sent Monte home for two weeks, Riggs went off to the *Saratoga* and Healy remained on base under the eye of Admiral Tunner."

Powell frowned, but said nothing.

"Riggs managed to obtain a three-day pass and made a detour to Milan. I wired him to proceed immediately to Gaeta and from there he will be flown back here."

"Do you think Riggs is in danger?" Powell asked.

"I hope not, but I think he is. I did not alert our people over there for reasons that will become obvious."

"None of this, Captain, is obvious."

"Sir, according to what was found in the wreckage, and from the travel section at Roosevelt Roads, there was another passenger on the plane besides Cob: a Marine major named Sanders. Admiral Tunner gave me his name and his serial number and I had one of my men run a check on him . . . No such individual has been assigned to Roosevelt Roads within the last ninety days and his service number belonged to a Major Sanders who was killed in Vietnam during the 1968 Tet offensive."

"Are you certain?"

"Absolutely."

"Goree, I want a complete report on the findings of the investigation team on that crash—and I want two of our *own* people to go down there this afternoon as soon as we finish here."

"Yes, sir."

"You haven't said anything about Admiral Tunner," Powell commented.

"The travel order for Major Sanders came from Admiral Tunner's office," Richard said quietly. This was where the ground became really treacherous.

"Are you—never mind. Go on," Powell snapped. "But be *very* careful, Captain."

"Before Cob boarded the plane, he radioed me the photographs and a transcript of the tape. My secretary signed for them. I examined them and positively identified the blister markings of a submarine exactly like the *Barracuda* and the *Bluefin,* and placed them in my office safe . . ." For the next three quarters of an hour, Richard went on to explain everything that had happened. He left nothing out. He told about his attempts to get Hopper, his wife's cryptic messages, and then the note he had found. He related how he had met Edwards earlier that morning, what Edwards had overheard at his weekly poker game—and that Edwards had been shot to death sometime before 1200, on his way to meet him at the Pentagon. He told them about Donna and her "hoodlum" attack. He explained about Gibbs, Captain Morris's relationship to the CIA, and the sale of the *Shark* to Chile. He talked about Crawton and Eastham. He mentioned the goblin sighting that morning. And finally he told the Admiral, "Sometime after 1200 I received a phone call from a man—" He stopped to clear his throat. "I was told they had my son . . . I was told to back off."

"You mean your son has actually been *kidnapped?* Did you contact the FBI?"

"No, sir. For security reasons, I did not want anyone from the Federal government or from the services to become involved. I turned the matter over to a New York City detective lieutenant I had been in touch with about the death of CPO Monte . . . I'm sorry, sir, but I found myself—"

"No need to explain," the Admiral said. "But your detective is going to need all the help he can get. I'll worry about the security."

Powell lifted the phone and put through a call to navy security in New York and told the officer in charge about the kidnapping and to immediately contact Lieutenant— "Fioredeliso," Richard said—of the New York City Police. "Put as many of our people at his disposal as he needs," Powell ordered. "If Fioredeliso has any questions, have him call me. I want you to move on this the *moment* I hang up . . . Yes, keep me informed."

"Thank you," Richard said.

"Let's hope we can nail the bastards," Powell replied. "Now, we have another problem to deal with."

"Yes, sir."

"Do you have Hopper's note?"

Richard handed it to him, and Powell looked at it for a long moment.

"What you're telling me is almost incredible, you realize that, don't you?" Powell said slowly, as if the words he spoke caused him great pain. "You're saying that there is a conspiracy in the Navy, a conspiracy very possibly aimed at overthrowing the *government* of the *United States.*"

"Yes, sir—in the Navy, and in conjunction with an outside group, as well. This man Gibbs and Captain Morris's former association with the CIA seem to point that way . . . Uh, sir, if you don't mind my saying so, right now the *Barracuda* is afloat and is—"

Powell waved him silent and, picking up the phone, dialed Captain Simione's number in the Operations Room. "Ask him about the goblin spotted by our number forty-seven," he said, handing the phone to Richard. He turned on the voice box so he and Goree could listen to the conversation.

Simione answered the phone.

"This is Captain Richard—"

"What can I do for you now, Captain?"

"Have you gotten any other ID on that goblin spotted by our forty-seven?"

"Are you pulling my leg?"

"No. I asked you if—"

"Captain, you called me yourself at 1235 and told me to scrub the goblin. I have it entered in my log . . . I asked you why and you gave me an ID. You said it was a Frenchy. What's going *on* up there?"

"Nothing, Captain, nothing, thank you very much. Things have been kind of frantic up here today. I have a note to call you and I forgot that I already took care of it. My apologies, and thanks again." He handed the phone back to Powell, who put it back on its cradle and turned off the voice box.

"I never made that call," Richard said.

Powell leaned back. His face had become very red. "Damn," he said softly to himself, "damn." Then, more loudly, "There's little chance we'll ever see Hopper alive. He'd be no good to them . . . sooner or later they'll have to kill him."

Richard nodded.

"How does this all look to you, Goree?" Powell asked.

"I wish I could say that I disagreed with Captain Richard," Goree said. "But everything seems to fit together. There's just one thing,"—he looked at Richard—"you haven't told us why, or rather *what,* they intend to do with the missiles."

"Fire them . . . at us . . . at the Russians . . . it makes no difference," Richard answered. "Either way, they start a holocaust. After that, I couldn't even begin to guess."

"No, my guess is they'll launch those missiles at Russian cities," Powell said. "It makes the most sense. If you were Crawton," he asked, looking at Richard, "where would you try to launch from?"

"Somewhere in the eastern Med, or the Aegean Sea. Remember, sir, with the hydrothermal detection equipment the *Barracuda*'s got, it could sit just about anywhere and hide from the sonar."

"Given its speed and its last sighting, where do you think it is by now?"

"Through the Strait."

"And when would it reach its optimum firing area?"

"I figured it out, sir, before I came over. I'd say by tomorrow 1400, our time."

Powell leaned forward and placed his elbows on the desk. "This has got to go all the way to the President," he said. "The *Barracuda* must be stopped. I'll get hold of Admiral

Darlin immediately to bring it to his attention."

Admiral Darlin's number was busy.

Powell put the phone down and for several moments none of them spoke.

Richard felt oddly guilty. The men involved were fellow officers. By discovering what had happened to the *Barracuda,* he had betrayed them. Almost as if he were reading his thoughts, however, Powell said, "You did the right thing, the only thing you could have done."

"Thank you, sir."

Powell turned to Goree. "Nothing about this entire incident must ever get out. I mean absolutely *nothing.*"

"Yes, sir."

"Now, I want you to place Captain Gray, Captain Morris and Admiral Tunner under *immediate* surveillance. Locate Mister Gibbs, if you can, and watch him too. As for Senator Eastham, I'll pass him on to a friend of mine at the Bureau."

"Is there anyone else?" Goree asked, looking at Richard.

"No . . . perhaps—"

"Go ahead," Powell said.

"Admiral Hays," Richard said. "I never had any direct contact with him about the *Barracuda,* but—"

"Add Hays," Powell ordered. "Richard, I want you to go about your ordinary routine—but wherever you go, leave a phone number and an address where you can be reached. We're going to need you. And watch yourself. Goree, cancel all your plans. For the next twenty-four hours, I want you in this office." He looked back to Richard. "And try to *relax,*" he said. "That may sound silly, but we need you in good shape. Right now you've done all you can. Now it's up to the rest of us."

Richard stood up and shook hands with Admiral Powell. As he left, Powell picked up the phone again to call Darlin.

When Richard returned to his office, Commander Smith was waiting. He beckoned to Smith to follow him, stopping first to ask if any additional news about Donna had come from the hospital.

"She's still listed as critical," the Wave said, "but the doctors think she'll make it."

Richard nodded and went into the office, Smith directly behind him.

"Close the door," he said, going to the desk. Three yellow phone message slips were there, one from Lieutenant Holmes, a second from Lieutenant Commander Carey. Neither had left a specific message, but both said they would phone back. The third came from Hilary. Please call. He set the message slips aside and dropped down into the chair. "Join me," he said.

Smith nodded and sat down.

"How did the meeting go?" Richard asked, filling his pipe.

"Admiral Hays and Captain Gray were absent. Each sent a replacement."

"Anything I should know about?"

"I made a note of all the important points . . . SubCom NATO had a report our sub number forty-seven had contact with a goblin this morning—but positive ID was made sometime later. By 1235 it had been given a French ID."

Richard nodded and sent a puff of smoke toward the ceiling. "That bandit was probably the *Barracuda,*" he said.

Smith started to speak, but Richard interrupted. "Don't ask any questions now."

"Yes, sir."

"Everything must continue as if nothing out of the ordinary is happening. I know you did it once, but caution all the personnel again about that. I want nothing mentioned outside this area about Donna or Captain Edwards . . . Now, I have another job for you. I want you to take three or four of our shore patrol people and go to Admiral Hopper's house. Put a guard there and make sure that *no* unauthorized personnel enter the house. Arrange with SP to keep the guard there until I personally sign their release."

"What about the Admiral's wife?"

"If she has any questions, have her call me, but I don't think you'll find her there. Thank you, Commander, that's all."

"Yes, sir," Smith said and left.

When the door had closed, Richard leaned back into the chair and closed his eyes. He had never felt so tense in his life. His head throbbed, his neck and shoulder muscles ached. *Relax,* Powell had said. God, how could he relax?

The sudden ring of his phone made him start, and he reached over to the intercom. "Could you find out who it is, please?" He wanted a few minutes of quiet, if he could get them, just a few minutes . . .

The Wave came back on. "Miss Hilary Gordon to speak to you, sir."

The sound of her name sent an immediate rush of desire through him. "I'll take it," Richard said, picking up the phone. "Yes, Hilary . . . I was going to call you," he told her without preliminary, "but stuff has been coming down here."

"Any chance for you to get away for dinner?"

He thought for a moment. Keep his activity normal, Powell had said, but what if they needed him? "I can't tell right now, Hilary, I'm pretty busy today—but I will if it's at all possible."

"Try," she told him.

"I most certainly will."

"I like the way you said that," she said. "It has the ring of authority."

Richard smiled. "I'll call later when I know better," he said. "But I can't tell you exactly when."

"I'll be here," she answered.

"I like the way *you* said that," he told her.

They said goodbye, he put the phone down and walked to the window. A premature twilight lay over the city. The cars on the highway had their lights on and lights were beginning to appear in the buildings across the river.

He remembered standing there only last evening, gazing out at the city as the rain came down. It seemed like a million years ago . . . He shook his head and returned to his desk just as his phone began to ring. "Captain Richard."

"Captain Richard, this is Admiral Powell. You are to proceed at once to the east entrance of the White House. Have all your papers with you and have all your calls routed through my office . . . And, Captain, it's not necessary for anyone on your staff to know where you're going."

"Yes, sir."

"I will see you there," Powell said.

The line went dead.

Richard put the phone down and took several deep breaths. This was it. The White House. He walked to the closet for his coat and hat, and on the way out told the

Wave at the desk he would call in later. "But in the meantime, if anyone should want me, put them through to Admiral Powell's office."

The girl nodded and he started to go, but her voice stopped him. "Uh, sir . . . some of us are going over to the hospital to see Donna tonight, and we collected some money for flowers . . . we thought you'd like to contribute."

Richard handed her a ten dollar bill. "If you need any more, please ask."

The lobby of the Shoreham was crowded with groups of noisy tourists, some of them being readied by their guides for late afternoon tours of Washington, others chattering about what they'd seen. Some of them might even be from his own state, Senator Eastham considered.

Ordinarily, he might have sought out one or two of the most prosperous looking men, and if they came from Mississippi, invite them for a drink. He had an almost unfailing intuition when it came to judging a man's financial status, and as an astute politician, he realized the idea of having a friendly drink with a member of the Senate was too much of a temptation for almost anyone to resist—no matter what his political persuasions might be.

Ordinarily, too, Eastham smoked a huge black cigar. Over the years, his cigar had become so much a symbol of his Senatorial power that political cartoonists had taken to depicting it larger than the Senator himself.

But he was not smoking the cigar now, nor was he looking to gladhand any Mississippians. Instead, he was hiding behind the open pages of the *Washington Post,* from time to time glancing nervously over the top, hoping to catch a glimpse of Gibbs returning to the hotel. Eastham had phoned Gibbs's room more than a dozen times since receiving Crawton's call and that had been slightly before noon. He had even left several messages at the desk to cover the possibility of missing him in the lobby.

For the first time in his long political career, Eastham felt the ground giving way under him. It was like standing in a bed of quicksand with nobody nearby to throw him a rope, his weight sinking him deeper and deeper. When he had first listened to Crawton's plans for bringing about a change in the government, he had seen them only as a highly accelerated version of his own ideas. Sooner or later, he had felt, there would have to be an East-West showdown —and the American government as it was now constituted would never be able to sustain such a confrontation. The only logical course was to change the government, make it stronger, its leader more powerful, with the military taking a much more active role in domestic and foreign matters. He saw himself playing a vital part in that type of government: if not the actual leader, then something very close to it, perhaps a sort of prime minister.

When Crawton had come to him with his particular plan, Eastham had immediately seen the possibilities, as had many of his friends. Gibbs and the others, in and out of the Company, had thought of everything. Absolutely every contingency, every emergency had been considered in advance—or so it had seemed. He still didn't understand what had happened in the last thirty-six hours.

He was not yet wholly ready to admit it, but the situation was becoming very frightening. It was one thing to feel in control of his own and other people's actions, but it was something else entirely to sense that control slipping away, passing from himself to strangers and the rush of events . . .

At ten minutes after three, Gibbs finally entered the hotel lobby. Eastham's first impulse was to throw the paper to one side and rush over to him, but with an effort he brought himself under control. No sense attracting attention. Besides, you never knew when there were reporters about. Eastham had learned a valuable lesson from the Watergate affair: never trust a member of the press—unless you had him in your pocket, or one of your friends did.

Eastham stood up slowly, folded his newspaper, and, tucking it under his arm, walked casually up to Gibbs.

"Why, Mister Gibbs," he said in his most courtly Southern manner, "it surely is a pleasure to meet you again."

Gibbs shook his hand. Despite the situation, he was feeling mellow. The roll in the sack with Hilary had turned into a strange and exciting sexual experience. He had had to use all his persuasive skills to overcome her reluctance . . . but he had been patient and had his reward.

"Would you care to join me for a drink?" Eastham suggested, adding *sotto voce,* "More trouble."

The smile immediately left Gibbs's face. He nodded, pulled his hand away from Eastham's and headed for the cocktail lounge.

As soon as they were seated, and a waitress in a miniskirt and low-cut peasant blouse had taken their orders, Eastham demanded, "Where in hell were you?"

"Getting laid," Gibbs said, smiling tightly. He didn't like being questioned by Eastham or any other creep.

"Crawton phoned," Eastham said. "Hopper is dead."

"What?" Gibbs started out of his chair, then quickly sat back down again. He looked about; nobody seemed to have heard. Hopper might have been valuable, not directly, perhaps, but certainly as a negotiable item when it came time

185

to take over the government. The Admiral's life would have been worth some concessions from the opposition.

Gibbs took time to light a cigarette before asking for the details.

"Crawton was there when it happened," Eastham began.

Just then the waitress came, and Gibbs waved him silent until she had put down the drinks and was well out of earshot.

"It's a lot worse than—"

"Will you please tell me what the fuck *happened,*" Gibbs told him. "Just give me the *details.*"

Eastham turned very red. He wasn't accustomed to being spoken to that way. "If you'll give me a chance, *Mister* Gibbs . . . Apparently Hopper killed one of the guards, took his revolver, killed another and got hold of his rifle. After that it was—"

"Yeah, I know what it was," Gibbs answered with an undisguised disgust in his voice. "I hope they had enough sense to get rid of the bodies."

Eastham nodded. Though he had known Gibbs for some time before becoming involved in all this, he suddenly realized he hadn't known the man at all. It was as if he were seeing Gibbs for the first time. The man sitting across from him was not working for Crawton or him, as Eastham had thought; nor working for the cause, as the officers on the *Barracuda* were; nor for any particular personal gain. Gibbs was in it because he was a professional killer who had found his place in the world.

Gibbs stubbed out his cigarette and took a long haul at his drink. "I should have known things would start to foul up as soon as Captain Crawton went screwing around Rio —but no, I let myself be conned by his old man into thinking that once Junior was aboard the sub, everything would be jimdandy . . . I should have hit the abort button right then." He downed the rest of it. "Well, this time I'm not going to let myself be conned."

"What are you going to do?" Eastham asked.

"It's too late for the abort button," Gibbs said. "I told Crawton what I would do if there were any more fuck-ups, and I'm going to do it."

"But—"

Gibbs bent closer to the Senator, his eyes narrowed to slits. *"Look,* Senator, there are only two ways this whole thing might not go down the tubes. One is if the sub does the job before we're discovered—and that, from where I sit, seems a bad bet. Two is if those of us who are *smart* enough pull out before it's too late. If we pull out and the sub makes it, we're still in a position to do what we set out to do."

"But what are you going to do *now?*"

"Nothing. If the Company is called on to help locate the sub, we'll do it to the best of our ability."

"But what about us? What about me?"

"That doesn't come under our charter," Gibbs answered with a smile. "Oh, don't worry, Senator. You're too valuable to our people. You'll be clasped in the protective embrace of the Company, as they say. Should it come to any revelations, we'll take care of you."

"How?"

"Simple. You infiltrated the cabal and at *great* risk to yourself gave us information that allowed us to track them down."

"And Crawton?"

Gibbs turned his thumbs down. "He and a few more will

187

have to be sacrificed. But we'll leave a few, a kind of nucleus for the future."

After a long pause, Eastham agreed, almost visibly shaking.

"And I wouldn't try to warn Crawton," Gibbs said, looking straight at him. "I'd become very upset if you did."

The way he said it sent a chill down Eastham's spine. He downed his bourbon, hoping it would bring some warmth to his chilled body.

Gibbs beckoned to the waitress and paid her for the drinks. But he made no motion to leave. Slowly, he said at last, "But you know, Senator, there *is* one thing I'd like to do before we retire from the field. Richard, that son of a bitch, Richard. He's been the burr in my ass all along—and he's the only one with enough pieces in his head to really put the finger on any of us. If we take that smug bastard out now . . . you and I and this little project of ours might still be in the ring someday." Gibbs grinned suddenly. "Oh, yes, that'd be real nice . . . What do you say, Senator, you want to come on a little job with me? Help save the old U.S. of A.?"

Eastham forced himself to smile.

Friday, November 17th. Ship time: 2300. It was most definitely a mistake to tell the crew anything. Tension is extremely high and several fights have broken out among the men. The worst of these brawls resulted in the knifing of a petty officer, Third Class Peter Smyth. The wound is serious and he is not expected to live out the night. His attacker, Seaman First Class Oliver Ryan, is under arrest and naturally faces a court-martial, but this is not what distresses me most. From what I can make of the incident, it began when Smyth claimed we did not have the right to make a preemptive strike, and Ryan said that the Russians would do it to us if they could. He was right, of course, but words led to blows and then came the knife. The other incidents were less serious, but all of them resulted from differences of opinion about our mission.

To keep the crew under stricter discipline, I have armed several loyal men with billy clubs to patrol the ship and act as a police force in the event of any future disturbance. The crew resents this, but it is absolutely necessary for the success of the mission.

What hurts me most, though, is how any of them can doubt the rightness of our mission. What kind of Americans have we been breeding? I blame it all on the schools and the press. The softness has been allowed to remain too long.

Within two hours we will be through the Strait of Gibraltar. We will stay close to the African coast and then follow the deep trench that runs east-west across the Med. I estimate we should be in firing position in approximately fifteen hours. If we do not reach the Aegean Sea, we will fire from wherever we are. The missiles will be re-targeted once they are on their course.

More and more I am beginning to see the strain on myself and my other officers. Tad looks as if he has aged twenty years. The others, too, have aged greatly in the past months. I have not heard one of them laugh since we were sighted by the recon plane. Even the conversation between them has fallen off considerably. They have withdrawn into themselves. I, at least, have this tape recorder to speak into. If we should survive, I will recommend all of them for the Navy Cross.

I have scarcely slept six hours in thirty-six, and

when I have slept, it has been for no more than ten minutes at a time. I find myself thinking about my father and my mother. I never knew my mother. I was told that she died when I was very young. When I was about fourteen, however, I discovered several packets of old letters. In one of them, the writer—I do not even remember his name—expressed his sadness to my father that my mother had seen no alternative left but to take her own life. I thought about that letter for years afterwards, but I never mentioned it to my father. Perhaps I should have? Perhaps, if I have the opportunity in the not-too-distant future, I will . . .

As we draw closer to our firing point, I find myself wondering if I am afraid of dying. I have never really known fear and I have lived through many situations where I could clearly see the fear in the faces of those around me. The circumstances of this mission, however, are very different from those of any previous one.

I have no doubt about the rightfulness of our purpose and this faith, of course, sustains me. But I would have to be candid with myself and admit that fear twists around in the pit of my stomach. Perhaps if we had not been spotted by the recon plane, I would not feel this way, but I know, and so do my officers, that we were photographed and though we never speak about it, we know that, according to the laws of the present government, we have committed piracy and high treason. I hope and pray that the people ashore are doing everything in their power to block or destroy the use of the photographs.

My great concern now is that some member of the crew will attempt to sabotage some part of the submarine. Now that they know what our mission is, several among them might not be willing to be

responsible for the death of so many, and might
take it upon themselves to do something to stop us.
I am doubling the watch among those whom I
know to be loyal.

I find it more and more difficult to keep a coher-
ent line of thought. My mind keeps leaping from
one idea to another. I suppose that is because I
have not slept for so many hours. I have nothing
else to say for now.

End of entry . . . Captain Crawton, Commander
of the submarine *Barracuda* . . .

As soon as Harris arrived at the Hotel la Scala in Milan,
he was told by the desk clerk to call overseas operator 27.
Within ten minutes of closing his door, he was speaking to
Mr. Henderson, of Scarboro and Henderson, Business Consultants.

"How's New York?" Harris asked.

"Weather's become worse," Henderson told him.

"Are you getting it from the south?"

"There's some sort of heavy weather over Washington
. . . Yes, I'm told it's very bad there."

"Sorry to hear that."

"Don't stay away too long," Henderson said.

"Can't afford to," Harris replied.

They said goodbye and Harris put the phone down. He
walked to the window and looked out at the Piazza della
Scala, dominated by the statute of Leonardo da Vinci. Beyond the statue, on the far side of the piazza, was Palazzo
Marino, the city's town hall. Two of its windows were
illuminated, but the rest of the building was completely
dark. A light snow had fallen that afternoon. Under the full
moon, it looked like a white carpet.

He moved away from the window and went to the other side of the room, where he had set his valise down. He opened it and removed a .38 caliber snub-nosed revolver, fitted a silencer to its muzzle, loaded it and put the safety on, then tucked the revolver into his belt. Taking a small medicine bottle from his shaving kit, he pried open the top and picked out an orange pill. He swallowed the pill with half a glass of water, and dropped down on the bed to wait for the drug to restore his flagging energy.

Harris closed his eyes. He felt exhausted. The effects of the last forty hours had taken a toll, he knew, and though he had gotten some sleep on the way over, it was not enough to compensate for the drain. Besides, he never really felt comfortable on a plane. Everything was taken out of his control. He had to rely on the skill of others and he was not the kind of a man who could do that with any degree of ease.

Soon the weariness that had started to engulf him began to lessen and he opened his eyes. Sitting up, he reached for the phone, and, in passable Italian, asked the desk clerk if Commander Riggs was in his room.

"No, signore, the officer has gone to the evening's performance at La Scala," the clerk told him.

"When will the performance be over?"

"At about midnight."

Harris thanked him, put the phone down, and glanced at his watch. It was eleven P.M. He had about an hour to decide where to kill him.

Harris left the hotel and walked to the base of the statue in the middle of the Piazza della Scala. From there he could see the brightly illuminated front of the opera house, much smaller than he would have suspected it to be. Harris weighed his chances for getting a round off and losing himself in the crowd—the silencer guaranteed there would be nothing more than a loud pop—but he was aware of the many policemen in the vicinity and there was always the chance of someone seeing the gun in his hand. Besides, though he had carefully studied Riggs's photograph on the way over, there was a possibility he might not be able to recognize him with so many other people around. Harris decided that attempting to take Riggs out in the street would be much too chancy. He looked back at the hotel. It was the only place to do it.

He nodded and rather than walk directly back to the hotel crossed to the far side of the piazza, made a right turn, and wound up on a colonnaded street across from the Duomo. He saw the restaurants there and suddenly realized how hungry he was. Well, he had a little time. He went into the Galleria and sat at one of the inside tables for a cup of espresso and a piece of pastry.

By the time he returned to the hotel, it was 11:45. He went to the telephone booth, dialed the hotel's number and asked for Commander Riggs. The operator told him there was no answer, but upon request told him that the Commander occupied room 407.

Harris went directly to his room. He removed his coat and picked up two pieces of white plastic. Each was six inches long, an inch wide, as thick as a credit card. He thought for a moment about taking one or two other tools, but decided against it after examining the lock on the door of his room.

Harris switched on the radio, kept the light burning and very quietly slipped into the hallway, from where he made his way up the steps to the fourth floor and quickly located

Riggs's room. It took one try with one plastic strip to slip the lock. He was inside the room and had the door closed within forty-five seconds.

The lamp beside the bed was on, Riggs's suitcase open on the floor, his shaving kit on the dresser. Next to the shaving kit was a cablegram.

Harris picked it up and brought it close to the lamp near the bed. It was from Navy Intelligence in Washington.

> Travel orders changed. Three day pass cancelled.
> Report to Gaeta Hq. for further orders.
> Signed Cap. Nathan Richard,
> Dept. Dir. Nav. Int.

Harris stuffed the paper into his pocket, went back to the dresser and put the envelope into his pocket. Then he looked around the room. He saw immediately the best place to wait was directly opposite the door, facing it. He picked up one of the chairs, moved it there and sat down. Riggs shouldn't be back for a little while yet, he figured. No one went right home after the opera.

He sat with his back to the window. From the increased noise outside, it sounded like the performance was over. Good, he should be done soon then. Harris was anxious to be on his way home, to be in America when the shooting started. Next to this operation, his work in Angola and Chile had been small time. Gibbs had even assured him an important place in the new security apparatus of the nation once the government came into the hands of men like Rear Admiral Crawton and Senator Eastham.

The noise outside dwindled to a few honking horns and the rumbling of tandem trolley cars every ten minutes or so.

Suddenly, Harris had to urinate. Damn. Well, make it quick. He left the chair, went into the bathroom, and was just finishing when—

Footsteps in the hallway.

He started back to the chair, but Riggs was already at the door.

Harris stopped. He was to the right of the door. When it opened, he wouldn't be able to see Riggs until the door was at least halfway closed. There was nothing he could do about it now. He drew the revolver from his belt and removed the safety.

Riggs put the key in the door, turned the lock and swung open the door.

The light from the hallway flashed over Harris. He squeezed the trigger, the revolver bucked—

Alerted by that one flash of Harris, Riggs dropped to one side, then sprang at him, grabbing for the gun.

Harris threw punches with his left hand, but they seemed to have no effect on Riggs. Breathing hard, the two of them crashed against the wall, bringing down one of the pictures. Riggs stayed close to him, slamming the back of Harris's head against the wall. The pain blurred Harris's vision. He could feel the blood begin to ooze down the back of his neck, and hear people in the hallway; they were shouting.

Suddenly, the revolver was between them and Harris felt the end of the silencer against his chest. He tried to push it away, but the next instant he felt a stabbing pain in his chest. Blood was in his throat. He staggered. The gun was torn from his hand. He fell onto the bed.

Riggs held the gun.

"Never should have happened," Harris said, shaking his head. "Never should've gone to piss." He rolled off the bed to the floor, where he lay dying . . . No one moved to help him. It was taking longer for him to die than he would have wanted. But he knew that was because he had lost control of the situation. . . .

A Secret Service agent was at the east entrance to the White House. As soon as Richard identified himself to the guard, the Secret Service agent stepped forward and said, "I'll take him, Bill."

The guard nodded.

"Come this way," the agent said.

Richard followed him into the White House and through the entire length of the building to the west wing. They walked very quickly. Finally, the agent stopped and knocked on a door.

"Come in," a man called from the other side.

The agent motioned him forward, Richard put his hand on the knob, turned it and stepped into the room. Everything seemed to stop for a moment. He was in the Oval Office. Richard looked around the room and quickly recognized the members of the Joint Chiefs of Staff and Admiral Powell, who came forward now to greet him.

"That was good timing, Captain Richard," Powell told him. "I've just explained the situation to everyone present, but I thought you could tell them some of the details I may have missed."

Powell escorted Richard to the President, who had come forward. Somehow, in the confusion of faces, Richard had missed his, though he couldn't see how. "Mr. President, permit me to introduce Captain Nathan Richard."

President Harry Andrews was a big, strapping man with wispy white hair and sharp gray eyes. He stuck out his hand

and said, "I'd rather have met you under different circumstances, Captain, but even so, I'm honored."

"Thank you, sir, but the honor is mine."

The President smiled and, gesturing to the Joint Chiefs, said, "This is Captain Richard, gentlemen, and that civilian lurking in the corner behind you, Captain, is Secretary of State Roy Blakely."

Richard glanced over his shoulder. He had seen pictures of the Secretary many times, but never had any of them shown him to be the thin, frail man with the sad face who now smiled wanly at him.

"Now, suppose you tell us exactly what happened," the President said, leading him to an empty chair close to his desk. "But before you start, I want you to know how much I meant it when I said I was honored to meet you. Admiral Powell has told me about your son . . . I have children. I think I can understand your feelings. I've dispatched several Secret Service men to help your friend in New York."

"Thank you, sir."

"Now, Captain, please explain it all to us from the beginning."

Richard repeated, piece by piece, what he had told Admiral Powell, adding the fact that the bandit had since been taken off the display board in the operations room because someone had falsely identified it, using Richard's name.

"Do you think officers in other branches of the services could be involved?" Secretary of State Blakely asked.

"Not to my knowledge," Richard answered, realizing he had not seen the man move out of the corner, and yet Blakely was now standing about six feet away from him.

"Then you consider it strictly Navy?" Powell said.

"Yes . . . with some members of the CIA."

The President gave a deep sigh. "Incredible . . . incredible. We will obviously have to deal with this quickly. But first, gentlemen, the question is, what do we do about the *Barracuda?*"

"I don't think there's any question about it, sir. It must be stopped," Blakely said, adding in a much lower voice, "I hope before it's too late."

Chief of the Air Force General Storz stood up. Like the President, he was a tall, broad-shouldered man. "And just how in hell are we goin' to do that, Mister Secretary?" he asked, his Texas drawl loud.

"Find it, General," Blakely answered, not in the least intimidated by the man's thunderous voice. "If we *don't* find it, we're going to be at *war* with the Soviets. Do any of you gentlemen want to take the responsibility for that— for the millions of casualties on our side and theirs?"

None of them answered.

"I would appreciate your opinion, Captain Richard," the President said.

"Sir, I agree with Secretary Blakely. It must be found and, if necessary, destroyed," Richard replied. "There is no other way."

"Captain, there are one hundred and forty men aboard that submarine," Admiral Darlin, the Navy Chief of Staff, said. "And you speak of destroying them as if it meant no more than a snap of your fingers. I would hope a man in your rank would think a great deal more about the lives of his men."

Richard flushed. The room was very quiet.

"They would not be *my* men, sir," Richard answered with controlled anger. "I would not use *my* men as Captain Crawton is using the crew of the *Barracuda.*"

The President spoke up. "None of us think you would, Captain Richard. But the fact remains that there are one hundred and forty American sailors aboard the *Barracuda.*"

"Sir," Richard responded, "the people behind this operation have already killed a number of officers to protect themselves. The officers aboard that submarine are not—"

"Excuse me," Admiral Powell said, "but I think we must ask ourselves three questions. The first is why they would do something like this. To start a war, yes. But there is a more important and less obvious answer. And that is to take control of the government. I think we have all confronted that possibility in this room today. Next to these two alternatives, the loss of one hundred and forty men seems a small price to pay. Second question. *Can* we stop the *Barracuda?* We don't exactly know the answer to that at this time. It won't be easy to locate and we don't know exactly how much time we have. And that leads directly to the third question. Do we tell the Russians?"

"I was wondering when someone would come around to that," the President said. "Do I have an answer? I'd even settle for an opinion."

The room was suddenly filled with a swirl of angry voices. "Tell the Russians! We can't possibly—" "You don't seriously think—" "Mr. President"—it was General Storz— "if we tell the Russians, there's no telling *what*"— Through the middle of it, Secretary Blakely's voice cut like a knife. "The *more* people we have looking for that submarine, the more chance we have of finding her. It just might be possible to get Crawton to surrender."

"Captain," President Andrews asked, "do you think Crawton is the kind of a man to surrender?"

"No," Richard answered.

"From what I have heard about him here this evening," Andrews said, "I would agree with you."

"That's just what I mean," General Storz thundered. "If we let the Russians—"

"Gentlemen," the President called out, "I think we all agree by now that the *Barracuda* must be found and stopped." He looked around the room. There was silent agreement even from Storz and Darlin. "And since we seem to be of the opinion that Captain Crawton is not likely to surrender, then we must stop him any way we can. Therefore, I am directing the Air Force and the Navy to move the necessary planes and ships into the Mediterranean and surrounding areas and to *immediately* begin a sea and air search for the *Barracuda.* If she is found, every attempt is to be made to contact her commander and persuade him to surrender. But if that fails, she is to be sunk. Is that clear? I want that submarine destroyed before she destroys the rest of us. I will sign the necessary executive orders for the action. Furthermore, a federal warrant will be issued for every individual named by Captain Richard, including Admirals Crawton, Hays and Tunner. I want them held on a charge of high treason. And, gentlemen, I cannot emphasize too strongly that *all operations* are to be conducted with *optimum security.* I don't want a *word* of this to get to the press until we are ready. If we have to sink the *Barracuda,* we will work out some appropriate cover story. But it will be covered . . . Is that understood?"

It was.

"As to whether or not we notify the Russians," the President said, "I will make that decision when the time comes . . . Now I suggest you gentlemen start the wheels turning.

I want that sub *found.* Thank you for coming."

The officers stood up and started for the door.

"Captain," the President called, "if you don't mind, I'd like you to stay a while longer."

Richard stopped and turned around. President Andrews and Secretary Blakely were coming toward him.

"I'll stay close by," Blakely told the President. "I'm afraid it's going to be a long night."

"Let's hope it's going to be nothing more than that," Andrews answered.

Blakely nodded to Richard, shook his hand and mumbled something about "a damn good job," then hurried out of the room.

"Let's sit down and talk for a few minutes," the President said, gesturing toward a sofa and a couple of armchairs. He dropped himself down on the sofa and offered Richard a cigar.

"No, thank you," Richard said, seating himself across from the President. Andrews suddenly looked very tired, Richard noticed, the energy for which the man was famous seeming to drain out of him. For a moment, they sat that way, silent; then the President looked up. "What do you think our chances are for finding the *Barracuda?*"

"Not good, sir. It has very sophisticated equipment on board to prevent that . . . but we might get lucky."

"Lucky. I dis*like* leaving something like World War Three to luck, Captain."

"It was luck that put that recon plane near the *Barracuda* in the first place, sir."

The President nodded and blew a cloud of smoke that floated toward the ceiling. "You know, don't you, some of your fellow officers are going to consider you another

Judas?" he said. "I know because of my defense cutbacks, I'm not exactly too popular with a lot of them."

Richard nodded. He hadn't given much thought to it, but it had occurred to him.

"I won't be able to help you," the President said, "at least not in any direct way."

"I understand."

The President stood up. Richard followed and the two of them walked toward the door.

"By the way," the President asked, "did you vote for me?"

"No, sir," Richard answered.

The President laughed and slapped him on the back. "Because I was too liberal?"

"Yes, sir," Richard answered. "I didn't think you knew what you were talking about."

"And you were right." Pointing to the chair behind the desk, he added, "Nobody does until he sits there and comes face to face with reality—and believe me it's a reality beyond imagining. Beyond imagining . . . but I already said that, didn't I?"

They reached the door.

The President extended his hand. "I could make some sort of remark that might be worthy of the occasion, but I won't. I won't speak about my gratitude or the gratitude of the nation—assuming we all get out of this in one piece. I will only tell you, as one man to another, how much I respect and admire you."

"Thank you, sir," Richard answered, shaking the President's hand. "It's mutual."

Eastham was at the wheel. Gibbs sat beside him. Neither of them spoke. For the past hour they had cruised around the White House, waiting for Richard to come out. Before that, they had trailed him from the Pentagon, but the traffic had been too thick to kill him then.

Eastham could not believe what was happening. Back at the lounge, he had smiled weakly at what he had taken to be Gibbs's bad joke about his going along on the job, but it had soon become all too appallingly clear that Gibbs was serious. Deadly serious. "Senator," he had muttered under his breath, "I need two men for this, and there isn't time to get anyone else. I'm *sick* and *tired* of all your high-and-mighties pretending you can keep your skirts clean while we go out and do the dirty work for you, so I'm telling you —*you're elected.* Probably the most honest election you've ever had." With that, Gibbs had smiled, a smile which had left no doubt in Eastham's mind that the man was capable of anything now. He had gone along.

"I don't see the need for this," Eastham said. He had said the same thing at least five times before. "The damage has already been done."

Gibbs did not bother to answer. It was simple. Captain Richard had blown the whistle on them. His going to the White House had confirmed that beyond any doubt. He deserved to be blown away. And wouldn't that just stick in Hilary's craw now? A better man than me? No, baby, no one was better . . . he touched the gun in his hand. No one.

"I don't want any of this," Eastham said, suddenly pulling the car over to the curb and stopping it. "I'm telling you, Gibbs, I *can't* be—"

Gibbs pushed the muzzle of a revolver against the Senator's side. "Don't do that," he told him. "Don't start playing the good guy on me now."

Eastham glanced down at the gun and, his courage evaporating again, slowly eased the car away from the curb. "But you can't be sure he'll come out the same way he went in," he protested.

"I'm sure," Gibbs answered.

"Suppose he's armed?"

"I'll take my chances."

"But why? Why kill him now?"

"Will you shut the fuck up and *drive.* . . . Two big mistakes in the operation. Putting the Admiral's cretin son in command and not taking Richard instead of Hopper. The second was a bigger fuck-up than the first."

Eastham made no comment.

made two more runs around the White House and then as they turned down East Executive Avenue Gibbs spotted Richard's car. "Slow down," he ordered. "That's fine."

Gibbs fitted a silencer to the end of the revolver's barrel and lowered the window. "Just a bit faster," he said, raising the revolver into firing position.

They were alongside of the Captain.

Suddenly, Eastham shouted, "Hit the ground, Captain!" At the same time, he flung out his hand, smashing it against Gibbs's face.

The gun went off.

Gibbs's vision blurred. Blood poured from his nose. He could see Richard diving to the floor of his car. He struck Eastham across the side of his head with the revolver.

The Senator let go of the wheel and threw up his hands to ward off the blows. In an instant, the car swung into the other lane and smashed headlong into an oncoming vehicle, sending both of the cars hurling into the fence alongside the Treasury Building.

The steering column was thrust inward, driving the wheel into Eastham's chest, while Gibbs was thrown forward. His head smashed through the windshield, cutting his throat.

Traffic stopped in both directions.

As he drove slowly away from the White House, Richard's memory of the Oval Office was still a blur. Isolated details came back to him: the large fireplace at one end, a painting of a seascape above it, the French window directly behind the President's desk. And a tall grandfather clock with cylindrical brass counterweights . . . somehow that still stayed with him. But the rest . . . it would probably be days before he got his impressions sorted out properly.

He became aware of a car moving slowly behind him, then drawing alongside. He was about to turn and look at it, when a voice suddenly called to him to hit the ground.

Instinctively, he jammed on the brakes and dropped to the floor. A pop sounded, followed by the ping of a ricocheting bullet. Then came a screech as the car next to him apparently went out of control and slammed head-on into another vehicle. A second later came a second, greater crash.

Richard scrambled to his feet out of the car and saw the two had crashed against the fence of the building across the street. He was the first person to reach the wreck. With a shock, he recognized Eastham. He didn't know the other. But he saw the revolver.

The man in the second car had been thrown clear, and he lay on the ground, moaning.

Eastham started to speak, but his voice was very low. Richard bent close to him. "Don't say anything now," he said. "Whatever it is will keep."

The Senator shook his head. "Too much killing," he whispered. "Too much . . . I've no stomach for it . . . thought I did, but I was wrong . . . wanted to kill you . . . stopped him . . ."

"Who is he?" Richard asked.

"Gibbs . . . Gibbs . . . *Mister* Gibbs," the Senator answered. Blood suddenly poured out of his mouth and he lost consciousness.

Within minutes two radio cars came screaming up to the scene of the accident. The officers pushed their way through the crowd. "Look, that guy has a gun in his hand," one of them said.

Rather than become involved with the police right then, Richard decided to leave his car there and eased his way out of the circle of people. Time enough to explain later. If there was a later. He turned his back on the accident and, walking up to New York Avenue, hailed the first empty cab he saw.

"Take me to the Pentagon," he told the driver.

"Do you know what's happening on Pennsylvania Avenue?" the driver asked. "Traffic is all blocked up there."

"No," Richard said. "I don't know anything about it."

The cabbie shook his head. "If it's not one thing, it's another. No matter where you drive, you can't beat the traffic in this damn city."

Richard said nothing. They made the rest of the trip in silence.

Saturday, November 18th. Ship time: 0130. We cleared the Strait at 0105, and at 0108 received a radio message on our assigned frequency, informing me that our purpose is known and much of our shore-based organization dismantled. I hope and pray my father escaped being hurt. It would surely kill him to stand trial for the crime of high treason against a country he loves so very much.

When I handed the message to Haywood, his face went white. And in a very low voice, he asked, "Oh my God, what are we going to do?"

And I answered, "We will do what we set out to do. Now it is more important than ever for us to be successful."

Haywood did not answer. Then he reported the death of Petty Officer Third Class Peter Smyth at 0139. This means Seaman First Class Ryan will have to stand trial for the crime. Though he continues his assigned duties, he is technically under arrest.

I appointed Haywood counsel for the defense and will act as presiding court officer myself. All the other officers aboard will either be members of the court, or function as the prosecutor on behalf of the Navy. We will follow all the regulations and abide by the Courts-Martial Manual.

Smyth's body must be stored in the refrigerator compartment until we are able to give it a proper burial. I have already written a special citation for the deceased, stating that he gave his life not only for the defense of his country but also for its high ideals.

At 0110, the communications officer informed me that there was a great deal of radio traffic around us, apparently deploying ships and planes along the entire length of the Med. He also said several attempts had been made to signal us, using our former frequency and code letters. No answer was transmitted, of course.

We are now being hunted by our own forces. There is a certain amount of pleasure in knowing that, for if our attack is successful and what is left of the organization ashore assumes control of the government, then I am sure I will be ordered to take command of all the American naval forces in this area. To command them, after having been hunted by them, will give me great satisfaction.

If I close my eyes, I can easily visualize the movement of the *Barracuda* through the water. It is a swift, steady movement. Almost completely silent. Our electronic devices guide us and we are invisible from above and practically immune from attack, thanks to our new sensing equipment.

Twelve more hours . . . God, give us twelve more hours.

To keep the entire crew at peak efficiency during this critical period, I ordered battle stations at 0115. We will not secure from battle stations until after we have fired our missiles.

I find it strange at a time like this, when all of my thoughts should be totally engaged with the success of this mission, that I also find myself thinking about sex, a particular woman that I have been intimate with. Perhaps it is the closeness of death that makes me reach out for life . . .

I am concerned about my father.

I have run out of words . . . I am extremely tired.

End of entry . . . Captain Crawton, Commander of the submarine *Barracuda* . . .

Lieutenant Fioredeliso was a short, dark, black-haired man with twenty years on the police force, half of those as a detective. He had reached the rank of lieutenant through sheer ability; certainly he hadn't made it easy for himself. He'd been a maverick in his ways too long to get the kind of automatic promotions other good guys did. Maybe that was the reason he'd never gotten married either. He had also had enough experience with the "darker side of human behavior," as the shrinks said, to fill several good-sized books of abnormal psychology, he figured—and to recognize some of that behavior in himself. Criminal, cop, sometimes they were uncomfortably close . . .

The first time he had spoken to Richard, his intuition had told him the Captain was into some sort of shit that went far beyond police work. And then he had called again and said that his son had been snatched . . . Fioredeliso knew right then and there that something very heavy was going down—and he knew, too, that he was going to be part of it. To hell with regulations.

At first the results hadn't been too promising. He'd sent two of his men to the school and he himself had visited the boy's grandparents, but the best anyone could come up with was that just after 11:30—an early lunch hour or something —a kid had seen two men drive up in a black car, probably a Buick, call to the boy on his way home, open the door, and snatch him in. Jesus, didn't anyone teach kids about strange cars anymore?

There they'd stuck for a while, stymied by a lack of manpower and leads, until the call had come through into the precinct house from some other naval officer, offering him as many men as he wanted. Obviously, this thing wasn't so much a secret anymore in the Navy. Forty-five minutes later, there were ten heavies from navy security standing around in the precinct house waiting for him to tell them what to do—and a few minutes after that, three Secret Service men. This shit really was deep.

By that time his Captain had become real curious about what was going on and Fioredeliso had lied his way through it, telling the old man all the play was connected with the death of Chief Petty Officer Monte. The Captain gave him a fish-eyed look, but said nothing.

Fioredeliso knew there were three ways the case could go if they didn't turn up any more leads on their own. The people who snatched the kid could get cold feet and let him go. They'd kill him and somebody would find the body. Or just possibly somebody might see the two men with the boy, sense something was wrong and telephone the police.

But, as it turned out, none of these things happened. Instead, sometime around 5:30, a call came into the precinct house, and a man's voice said, "The boy is at 323 Vine Street, Great Neck, Long Island." In order to give a man time to trace the call, Fioredeliso pretended—as was S.O.P. —to have difficulty hearing. The man repeated the address.

"Pine Street," the Lieutenant said. "Pine Street, right."

"*Vine* Street," the man shouted, exasperation—or was that a bit of panic?—creeping into his voice. "323 *Vine* Street."

"Vine Street," Fioredeliso repeated.

The line went dead.

"Do we have a trace on it?" Fioredeliso asked.

"From a paybooth number in the Pentagon," the technician told him. The Pentagon? Fioredeliso shook his head. He had been right after all. Somebody had gotten cold feet.

In minutes, the operation was set up. Fioredeliso, four of his men and the team from naval security set off for Great Neck. On the way, he radioed the local precinct, and by the time he arrived at the scene, a portion of Vine Street had already been cordoned off.

Teams of two and three men moved around the house, covering all its entrances. Fioredeliso figured there were at least two men inside with the boy. To minimize the risk, he set up a diversionary action.

Using a walkie-talkie, he carefully coordinated the movements of all fifteen men, and then sat back to wait. He considered evacuating the residents from the houses on either side, but there wasn't time—the movement and noise would be sure to alert the men inside. I hope to God no shots go wrong, he thought. That's all I'd need.

One of the Navy heavies reported two men inside in the living room, watching TV. But no sign of the boy.

"Are you sure there are only two of them?" Fioredeliso asked.

"That's all I see," came the answer.

Fioredeliso checked his watch. It was 6:45.

"Two minutes to go," he said, feeling the knot in his stomach tighten. He left the car, opened his coat and drew a snub-nosed .38 from inside his belt. Another glance at his watch. "Ninety seconds," he said quietly. "Sixty . . . forty . . . thirty . . . twenty . . . ten . . . go." He set the walkie-talkie down on the hood of the car and ran toward the house.

At the same time, a panel truck came roaring down the street and swung hard into the black car parked in front of 323 Vine Street. There was a screech of brakes, followed by the gunning of an engine. The black car crunched onto the curb.

The door to the house sprang open, and a man shouted, "Someone hit our car!" He ran toward the curb.

The second man was in the doorway.

"Holy Christ, Hal, the whole back end—"

Hal made it halfway toward the car before Fioredeliso shouted, "Police, freeze." Several powerful searchlights came on. The man nearest the car reached for his gun.

Fioredeliso pulled off two rounds in quick succession: the

first struck the man in the shoulder, the second hit him in the chest.

The other man put his hands up.

Fioredeliso ran forward. "Where's the boy?"

"In the bedroom. Don't shoot!" the man said. A dark stain ran down his pants.

"Get this guy away from me," Fioredeliso said, disgusted, and went into the house. Moments later he found the boy, tied hand and foot and lying on a bed. "Bastards!" Fioredeliso swore softly. He cut the ropes and lifted the frightened boy in his arms. "Come on, Henry, you're going to be all right. I'm going to take you home to your grandmother and grandfather."

The boy looked at him and then hugged him tightly, more tightly than Fioredeliso had ever been held in his life. After a moment, to his surprise, Fioredeliso hugged him back.

Halfway to the Pentagon, Richard changed his mind and told the cabbie to take him to the Grass Hut instead. He needed a few minutes to get rid of the knot in his stomach, to unwind for just a little while from the grueling pressure of the last several hours. He wondered for a moment if he was still in danger, but decided, no, this had probably been it.

Though it was already well into the cocktail hour, the Grass Hut wasn't crowded, which was the way he liked it. The jukebox was playing some syrupy instrumental piece as Richard found a place for himself at the bar.

Sylvester, down at the other end, nodded to indicate he'd be with him as soon as he finished pouring martinis for two other customers. Richard motioned to him that he was in a hurry, and began to nibble on some peanuts.

It was a very strange feeling—almost being killed. He had been close to danger many other times during his career; he'd even been depth-bombed once by two Russian destroyers as he was probing the defenses in the waters around Murmansk. Those hours under attack had been a sweaty, agonizing ordeal—but somehow this was different. Someone had been shooting at *him,* only him. It was so much more personal.

"How're all the ships at sea?" Sylvester asked with a grin.

"Afloat," Richard answered flatly.

"Are you okay?" the barkeep asked. "You look worse than you did last night."

"Thanks."

"It's part of my friendly manner," Sylvester said, pouring a double shot of Scotch. "That's on the house."

"I ought to look terrible more often," Richard responded, gesturing toward him with the glass before he downed the Scotch in two swift belts. The quick spread of warmth in his body felt good. "I'll have another."

"Double?"

"Better make it a single," Richard replied. "I still have to go back to the office." He took longer drinking that one. When it was finished, he asked Sylvester for a dollar's worth of change and, sitting down in the phone booth, dialed Hilary's number.

After three rings, she answered.

"I'm still not sure if I'll be able to make it," he said.

She laughed. "That's no way to begin a phone conversation. I might have mistaken you for someone else."

"Not likely," he said. "I'm the man with the tired-sounding voice."

"As bad as all that?" she asked.

"Worse. I passed *as bad as all that* hours ago."

She laughed again.

"You know, I don't think there's anything else I'd rather do now than listen to you laugh."

"Why, thank you, sir . . . Will I get to see you at all tonight?"

He felt a sudden rush of desire. "Tell you what, it's . . . six-thirty now," he said. "Why don't we make a reservation for dinner, and if there's any way I can make it, I will. If not, I'll give you a ring. Sound okay?"

"Anything you say sounds okay. How about the Sea Catch?" she suggested.

"That's fine. See you about eight-thirty?"

"Uh-huh. See you," she said in her low, sensuous voice.

Richard smiled and hung up, but remained seated in the telephone booth for a few moments. No woman had made him feel this good since Joan . . . Joan . . . she would have approved of Hilary, he was sure. Come *on,* Nathan, she would have said, you waiting for an engraved invitation? Why don't you—?

He shook himself suddenly and left the phone booth. What a time to be thinking of something like that. *If the Barracuda isn't stopped, there won't be any time left for me or for anyone else.* The thought made him hunch his shoulders as he walked back to the bar and asked Sylvester to phone a cab for him.

"Where to, Captain?" the barkeep asked, reaching back to the sideboard for the phone.

"Where else?" Richard answered. "The Pentagon. Home sweet home."

XV

President Andrews stood at the French windows behind his desk and looked out at the bare lawn. The smoke from his cigar made a thin, grayish-blue column that rose almost to the ceiling before it dissipated . . . Half his first term was over. He had no idea whether he'd be elected for a second four years. He wasn't even sure that he wanted to run. The last campaign had been grueling and he had managed to squeak by on less than fifty thousand votes. His critics claimed he was turning the country into a socialist state, while his supporters countered with demands for more and more government control. Somehow he'd managed to balance them all and do some of the things that needed doing, but if he had had any illusions when he assumed the Presidency, they had been stripped away from him in the early months of his administration.

The truth was—cliché or no—that no man *was* ever big enough for the job, which was why the President's own staff had grown over the years, and through many different administrations, into a small army of specialists. He depended on these specialists to brief him on everything from medical research to international affairs. But not one of them ever mentioned a word questioning the reported sinking of the *Barracuda* . . . He removed the cigar from his mouth and turned around to Blakely.

"Off the record," the President asked, "what do you think?"

"Our chances of finding it are very slim."

That wasn't the answer the President was looking for. He knew Blakely had purposefully dodged the question.

"I'd wait to hear the opinion of the others," the Secretary of State said now.

Andrews nodded. "I guess that's why I summoned them here." And he faced the window again. "At least the sky is clear," he said, looking up through the topmost panes. "I can even see some stars . . . You know, when I was a kid I thought about becoming an astronomer. I even built my own reflecting telescope."

"What changed your mind?" Blakely asked.

"I'll be damned if I remember." The President laughed.

"But this office is one helluva country mile from an observatory."

Before Blakely could answer, the phone rang and he answered it. "Yes, have them brought in." He put the phone down. "Our visitors are here."

"Both at the same time?"

"It can happen if you arrange it right." Blakely let a faint smile show on his lips. Then he picked up the phone and asked Douglas Freeman, the President's Chief of Staff, to come into the Oval Office.

Soon a knock came on the door, and they were ushered in: Senator Edward Dee from New York, the Senate Majority Leader, and Senator Thomas Koss from Ohio, the Senate Minority Leader.

Dee was forty-six years old, a devout jogger and tennis player, tall, handsome and easygoing—and one of the country's most astute politicians. It was no secret he was being groomed for the Presidency.

Koss was sixty. His family had been in the steel business for several generations. He was a compactly built man with steady blue eyes, a strong chin and soft voice. He made no bones about the fact that he believed the government should protect the rights of big business first, the military second and the general public last, as beneficiary of the first two. During his thirty years in the Senate, he had voted against every bit of social legislation that had come before that body.

Douglas Freeman joined them, bringing with him Harry Porter, the President's Special Adviser.

Freeman was thirty-five, a heavyset man with slightly prominent eyeballs, and renowned in Washington for his sense of humor. Porter was not on the Presidential staff. He was the President's former law partner from New York, fifty-three years old, tall, dignified and much respected by members of both parties.

"Well, gentlemen," the President said, "I appreciate your response. I hope I haven't inconvenienced anyone too much. Please make yourselves comfortable." He gestured toward the sofa and armchairs.

"Mister President," Koss said, choosing the sofa, "I have received word of considerable movement of our planes and ships in the Mediterranean. Does this meeting, by chance, have anything to do with that information?"

The President threw a brief glance at Blakely and then, looking at Koss, said, "Senator, as usual, your sources are impeccable. The information is entirely correct."

Koss was on his feet again. "Let me remind you, Mister President, that I and other members of my party have repeatedly warned you about the inadvisability of supporting Israel militarily. If we intercede in any conflict between them and the Arabs, we *must* be prepared to face another oil embargo. Frankly, Mister President, I don't think we can afford to pay that kind of price again."

President Andrews nodded and, in a low voice, said, "Thank you, Senator Koss. The price we may have to pay tonight might well make the price of oil and the whole question of the Middle East somewhat academic."

Koss looked nonplused. "Then what—?"

"Before I offer any further explanation," Andrews replied, "I would like to say to the senators first that their presence here tonight is in an advisory capacity to the President; that is to say, what I have to tell you and what I want from each of you has nothing to do with party politics."

Senator Dee's expression now matched that of Koss.

The other men, with the exception of Blakely, raised their eyebrows in a question, but tried to keep their faces expressionless.

The phone rang.

Blakely answered and, nodding, told the President that Admiral Darlin was in the building and would be with them shortly.

"In the meantime," the President continued, "I have a few other comments to make about the issues that will be discussed here. First, they must be regarded by all of you as absolutely top secret. Should the security of the matter under discussion during this meeting be breached or in any manner leaked to the press, I will use all the power of this office to determine the guilty individual and then make him regret it."

"Those are strong words, Mister President," Senator Dee responded. He shifted in his armchair. "I don't take kindly to being threatened, even by you, Mister President."

"I know they are strong words, but I meant exactly what I said," Andrews replied. "And I assure you, gentlemen, the situation requires them. All of you must decide here and now whether you will stay or leave this office. If you elect to stay, then be assured you must be bound by what I have said."

The men glanced at one another, but none of them made a move.

"Second thing," the President said. "If we survive—and that is a real if—many of the people we know and some of our friends will be arrested and tried for high treason and —no, let me finish, *please*—and I will need your support to introduce special legislation."

They were all talking at once now. "Mister President,"

Harry Porter broke through, "I know you want to put down the ground rules, but I think you'd better tell us what's going on. High treason?"

"Yes," the President said. "And more. The issue here is war, or rather the possibility of war."

"Mister President," Koss questioned, "have *you* ordered a preemptive strike?"

"No, Senator," Andrews answered. "I have not, but someone else has."

"You mean the *Russians* plan—"

"Senator, at this moment an American nuclear submarine is on its way to deliver sixteen MIRV missiles to the heartland of Russia."

"Oh my God," Dee said quietly.

Koss opened his mouth and then abruptly closed it again.

At that moment, the door opened and Admiral Darlin joined them. "They are not answering their call," he told the President.

"They," Andrews explained to the other men, "are the officers of the submarine *Barracuda.*"

Another babble of voices. "But she went down three . . . three and a half months ago!" Freeman said.

The President shook his head. "Unfortunately, gentlemen, we have found she did not. I'll explain in a moment. First"—turning to Admiral Darlin—"will you tell us something about the mechanics of launching a missile from a submarine? Tell us who is responsible for what."

Darlin, who had not had the opportunity to sit down, took several steps forward. "Mister President, I will limit my remarks to this particular situation. The missiles can be fired at any time by an order from the captain of the submarine. There is a key. A key that allows the captain to close one of four switches on the firing circuit. Launch control has a key. There is another control switch on the same circuit in the navigation center, the trigger for which is in the missile control center. A submarine, because of the nature of its operating environment, does not have a remote switch, known as a Permissive Action Link, to safeguard against unauthorized firing. A submarine is an independent entity."

"In other words, gentlemen," the President said, "What we have is an independent entity on its way to start World War Three."

"But how could that have happened?" Dee asked.

"I'll let the Admiral tell you."

Darlin was concise and very accurate. He explained everything they had been told earlier by Richard—"Senator Eastham!" Koss exclaimed—and when he was finished, turned to the President and added, "It seems Senator Eastham and Mister Gibbs are no longer part of the picture. They were involved in an auto accident not far from here. Admiral Powell has told me that Eastham is in critical condition and that Gibbs is dead. Powell intimated that Gibbs had made an attempt to kill Captain Richard after our meeting today. I'll have more details later."

"Is Captain Richard all right?" Andrews asked, shaken.

"Yes, he called Powell's office as soon as he returned to his own."

"Eastham," Koss said, shaking his head. "I still can't believe . . . treason, and now—I always thought him a patriotic—"

"I'm sure he thought the same thing," Blakely said quietly.

The others were silent, lost in their own thoughts. Finally, Senator Dee spoke. "And what is being done about the situation, Mister President?"

The President's cigar had long since gone out. He walked to his desk, took a fresh one from a mahogany humidor, cut the end, lit it, and returned to where the men were sitting. "I have ordered a massive search and destroy operation," he told them. "The *Barracuda* must be stopped."

Darlin, who had at last settled down in one of the empty chairs, moved a bit forward. "The missiles aboard the *Barracuda* will inflict some thirty million casualties on the Russians. I assume they would retaliate immediately from their Siberian bases and destroy most of the Northwest, northern California and possibly Los Angeles. Our losses in that should run in excess of five million casualties, if Los Angeles is included, then fifteen million. On another front, we could effectively neutralize their missile-carrying submarines in the Atlantic and off our West Coast. However, it is very likely the Russians would proceed to invade western Europe and Japan. If in the first seventy-two hours we could not hold them, or push them back, our estimation is that then we would be committed to a major land war."

"Could we hold them?" Dee asked, amazed at this calm discussion of the unthinkable.

"I think we might even be able to push them back," the Admiral answered. "We would have to depend heavily on our air power and missile strength, but we could do it."

"Wouldn't they do the same?" Freeman asked.

"Most definitely. But with less effectiveness, according to our information."

"Do *you* think we should notify the Russians?" Dee asked.

"No, Senator, I don't."

"So that was why there was so much ship and plane movement," Koss said.

"Yes."

"Well, then, since you've already taken action," Koss said, "I'm not sure I see why you asked us here. Furthermore, I'm not sure I wholly agree with the measures you've taken. After all, the enlisted men aboard the *Barracuda* are innocent of any crime, except obedience to their officers."

"Mister President," Dee began, "I think that some other way—"

"There is no other way," the President said. "I know that ɩhe enlisted men are guiltless, but they are in that damn submarine and there's no way to get them out." He was becoming annoyed and the sharpness of his voice showed it. "I didn't bring you here to discuss the actions I have already taken. I want to know what your opinion is on a completely different matter. More specifically, I want to know how you feel about notifying the Russians."

"The Russians!" Dee said.

"That's right, Senator. But before we proceed, I think we should understand exactly what our options are. Admiral, I'm sure you can explain them better than I can, at least from the military point of view."

"Because you think we have a very good chance of winning?"

"Yes," Darlin answered. "Because of that. And there's one more thing, too. If we told the Russians about the *Barracuda,* we would also have to tell them about its special instrumentation, which the Soviets have *not* developed yet, and about what cities are targeted for the missiles."

"In other words," Koss said, "we would be giving them

secret information that they might later be able to use against us?"

Blakely interrupted. "Of course they would have to know something about the nature of the equipment the *Barracuda* has aboard if they were going to—"

"Mister Secretary," Koss said, "are you seriously suggesting we allow the *Russians* to find and destroy one of *our* submarines?"

"Senator," Porter spoke up, "the *Barracuda* can no longer be considered one of ours. It is a pirate vessel."

"Furthermore," Douglas Freeman said, "this business about 'winning' the war. That's what the military told us about Vietnam, Admiral. Thirty million casualties, fifteen million casualties—you toss those figures around like they were nothing, but those are human *lives,* Admiral. Do you seriously think *any* nation could 'win' a Third World War? Look, Wordsworth wrote 'Winning or losing, we lay waste our powers.' *Lay waste our powers.* Can anything possibly be worth it?"

"But just suppose," Dee offered, "that the Russians are caught so far offbase that they *can't* retaliate. What I mean is what if we follow the *Barracuda*'s strike with an all-out military effort?"

The President raised his eyebrows.

"This may be a sort of blessing in disguise," Dee said.

"I would hardly call an initial casualty rate of fifteen million a blessing in disguise," Freeman replied, his voice rising.

"Mr. Freeman," Koss said, "perhaps blessing was the wrong word, but we all know what the Senator meant. I see an opportunity here that might never come again. We could be remiss not to take advantage of it. Mister President, I am against telling the Russians anything about the *Barracuda.*"

"As am I," Dee said.

Andrews looked toward Blakely.

"Mister President, we *must* tell them. The risk would be too great," replied the Secretary of State. *"Much* too great." Freeman and Porter agreed with Blakely.

"I take it," the President said, addressing Darlin, "that if I decide to withhold the information from the Russians, you would be ready to deliver additional strikes within minutes?"

"Yes, Mister President. We have the capability to totally neutralize any Russian counterstrike, if we act quickly."

The President nodded and shifted his cigar from the right side of his mouth to the left. "Gentlemen, I have listened to you all, and I have a lot to think about. Please accept my thanks for coming to this meeting on such short notice."

The men stood up.

"Can you give us some indication of what you intend to do?" Senator Dee asked.

"I haven't decided," Andrews answered the majority leader. "Admiral, how long do you estimate it will take the *Barracuda* to reach its optimum firing position?"

"By one o'clock in the morning, our time," Darlin answered, "she should be going into the Aegean Sea."

"That doesn't give me long to think," the President said quietly. Then, with a shake of his head, "It took God Almighty six days to make the world . . . I have less than that many hours to decide whether or not to let much of it be destroyed. God help me."

When he was finally alone, the President dropped down into the chair behind the desk. He was weary, more weary than he ever remembered feeling. He loosened his tie and opened his collar, and leaning back, closed his eyes. He felt like weeping, then, to his surprise, he suddenly lurched forward and, burying his face in his hands, he did weep.

"No man," he said out loud, "no one man should be given the power to . . . take the lives of so many people . . . No man should be able to do that . . ."

After a few minutes, he used his handkerchief to wipe his eyes and blow his nose. He stood up and decided to join his family for dinner, something he had not been able to do for several nights. . . .

Richard had put a call through to Admiral Powell's office immediately upon returning to his office, and related the details of his encounter with Gibbs and Eastham. "You're a very lucky man, Captain Richard," Powell had said. "And a very foolhardy one. I *told* you to stay out of danger. What were you doing driving alone? A man like Gibbs seldom misses his target. Now, this is what I want you to do," he had added. "I want you to go home"—Richard started to object—"I said, *go home,* get some rest, and stay secure. You've been up a long time now, and we can't afford to have lack of sleep clouding anyone's judgment. You've done all you can, Captain, now let us take over." Richard started to object again. "That's an *order,* Captain. Take off. Leave your phone number. If we need you, you'll be called, I promise you."

Richard agreed—actually, he thought, now he could make that dinner with Hilary—but he still couldn't leave, not just yet. Sometime after the night Duty Officer took over, Richard left his office and went down to Operations room, where the activity was frenetic.

Simione was still in command and when he saw Richard, he said, "Would you believe it? At 1600, every goddamn ship and plane in the Med was put on alert. There's a search and destroy operation going. I swear, I'd like to clobber the mother who thought this one up!"

Richard sympathized.

"All the stuff is real," Simione said. "The planes are carrying—hey, wait a minute! Do you know what's going on?"

"I heard you were busy," Richard answered with a straight face, "so I came down to take a look."

"Bullshit! You're the guys who are supposed to know what's going down. I *thought* there was something funny about all that business this afternoon."

Richard shrugged.

"All right, *don't* tell me! I know we're looking for a sub," Simione said. "But that's all I know. All our subs have been pulled back to the area inside those green lights on the status board—any sub outside that area is going to be in for one hell of a time, unless she gives her ID within two minutes after being contacted."

Simione excused himself then and made the rounds of the various slave computer terminals that fed information into the master computer controlling the display board. Suddenly, he turned and motioned to Richard.

"Captain, you have a call. Take it on the green phone."

"Captain Richard." Richard held the phone close to his ear, still keeping his eyes on the display board.

"This is Lieutenant Fioredeliso," the voice said. "There's someone here who wants to speak with you."

Richard's heart began to race.

"Dad, is that you?"

"Henry? Henry, yes, son, it's me. Are you all *right?"*

"Sure. I'm with grandma and grandpa and your friend . . . Are you coming home soon?"

"Soon!" Richard answered. He felt like singing. "Soon as you can imagine. Hey, maybe you'd like to come down here. Would you like that?"

"Dynamite!"

Richard laughed. "Okay! Hey, I can't talk too long now. I'll talk to you later. Let me speak to grandpa. I love you, Henry . . . Dad? Yes, dad, it's wonderful. Look, I can't tell you anything now, dad, and maybe not even later, but kiss mom and tell her everything will be all right. That's right . . . Me, too, dad . . . Now let me speak to the Lieutenant."

"I owe you," Richard said, when Fioredeliso was back on the line.

"We got lucky. Someone phoned in a tip."

"Who?"

"No idea," the Lieutenant said. "But it came from a phone booth in your building."

"What?"

"Someone who can make high level decisions."

"So it would seem . . ."

"The two guys who snatched your son turned out to be the two who snuffed CPO Monte."

"Any leads from them?"

"We're working on it."

"Thanks," Richard said. "Thanks again."

"I have a strange feeling that I should be the one who thanks you," Fioredeliso said.

They said goodbye, and Richard spent a few more minutes talking with his son before he put the phone back in its cradle. He gave a deep sigh of relief. His son was safe.

It was enough for him to know that now.

Richard crossed his arms and turned his attention back to the display board as the situation developed moment by moment. It looked like there were hundreds of planes involved out there and at least a hundred ships.

"Like looking for the proverbial needle in the haystack," Simione remarked, coming back beside him. Then he added, "The Russians are getting jumpy. They picked up our traffic out there and it looks like they're starting to move some of their own planes and ships around."

"I noticed the increase in red lights," Richard said.

"Happens all the time," Simione replied. "We move, they move. It's kind of a crazy tango, if you know what I mean."

"Yeah . . . I know what you mean," Richard answered. A wave of exhaustion suddenly came over him. "I think I'll call it a day."

"I wish I could do the same," Simione said and returned to his station.

"Think of it this way," Richard told him, "you might even be doing some good here."

"Not likely." Simione laughed.

Richard left the Operations Room. As soon as he stepped into the corridor, the smile left his face. His son was safe . . . but the *Barracuda* still remained. If it slipped through, the destruction would be catastrophic. But even if they caught it . . .

From his own experience, he knew what waited for the men in the *Barracuda*. If they were lucky, it would be over swiftly. But if not, they would lie on the bottom for hours, perhaps days, unable to escape the certain death that awaited them. Some would not be able to take the mental strain and would go crazy with fear. He had seen it happen aboard his own vessel. One of the junior officers had become so frightened, he'd turned into a child again. He himself had been terrified—

"I thought I'd find you down here." Captain Goree had approached from the other end of the corridor.

"I wanted to see how it was going," Richard answered.

"And how is it going?" Goree asked, falling into step.

"Busy. But nothing yet."

"I suppose it's too soon . . . By the way," Goree said, "just to show you how full of coincidences this world of ours is, I had one of my men in Roosevelt Roads question Commander Cob's wife today. It seems she was in Rio a while ago and spent some time with a man who fitted Captain Crawton's description. Later she made a positive ID from a photograph."

"Yeah, small world all right," Richard replied quietly.

"She didn't know he was a naval officer. He told her he was in the import-export business."

Richard shook his head.

"I think the press is on to something, Captain," Goree told him. "That's why I came down to see you. I thought it was time we came up with a cover story."

Richard agreed.

"Extensive maneuvers or a show of strength for the Middle East," Goree said. "Take your pick."

"I'll go with whichever one you choose."

"I like the Middle East," Goree said.

"Okay, the Middle East," Richard said. "But you know this whole damn thing is going to come apart anyway. If the *Barracuda* delivers her missiles, we will be involved in a war, and if we sink her and bring certain men to trial, the entire story of the cabal is going to come out. Not to mention Eastham's crackup today."

Goree said nothing.

"You know what I'd like, Goree? I'd like to wake up tomorrow morning and find out that has all been some long long nightmare. Just a bad dream . . . but it won't happen that way."

"It never does," Goree said. "At least not in our business . . . I think I should warn you. Crawton doesn't have many friends . . . but the ones he does have are in very powerful places. They're still around."

"I didn't think he'd bother with anyone less," Richard said. "But I understand what you mean."

"I thought you would."

They reached the exit. Richard said, "I gave the number where I can be reached to the night Duty Officer, but just so you know, I'll be at the Sea Catch for dinner."

"That's a good place."

"Yes . . . come to think of it, I'm starved. I don't think I had anything to eat all day."

"Go ahead, you deserve some time. You did one helluva job today," Goree said.

"In a way, I wish I hadn't . . . There are one hundred and forty men on that submarine, Captain, and they're all going to get it in the neck, guilty or innocent. Their only chance is if Captain Crawton surrenders and we know how much hope there is of that."

"Well, good night, Captain," Goree said. "If anything develops that you should know about, I'll give you a call, don't worry. And . . . well, I'm repeating myself, but for what it's worth, you *did* do a helluva job today."

Richard shrugged.

The two men shook hands.

Richard turned and walked out into the parking lot. More than anything in the world now he wanted to be with Hilary, to forget all this. Tomorrow, if there was one, he would find some way of having Hilary meet his parents and his son. He was sure the three of them would fall in love with her as quickly as he had.

The recessed fluorescent lighting fixture gave the Situation Room an almost antiseptic quality, an impression enhanced by the long light wood table in the center and the straight-back chairs around it. President Andrews sat at the head of the table. Blakely was on his right. Of all the rooms in the White House, it was the one he liked the least and he said as much to Blakely, as they waited for the other men to arrive.

"I wouldn't mind it so much," the President said, "if it had windows. But the way it's blocked off from everything else just *bothers* me."

"Indeed. You know in all the years I've known you," Blakely remarked dryly, "it has never occurred to me that you were the least bit outdoorsy."

Andrews glared at him for a moment, and then a smile began to crack on his lips. A moment later, it was gone, however, and his fingers resumed their nervous drumming on the table.

Porter and Freeman came into the room.

"For the time being, sit down anywhere, gentlemen," the President told them.

"Mister President," Porter said, "the press is on to something. They smell a big story."

Andrews nodded, but did not answer. He helped himself

to a cigar from the humidor at the end of the table and tried to will his insides to calm down. The roast veal he had eaten for dinner, along with everything else, seemed to be lodged somewhere between his throat and his stomach.

Admiral Darlin arrived and, within minutes, Senators Dee and Koss.

The President bid them move closer to the head of the table, then said, "I trust each of you has had time to have your dinner. I had mine, though to be honest, I wish I hadn't eaten as much as I did. Sitting at the table did give me the opportunity to see my family, though. I'm glad I saw them, very glad." He set his cigar down in an ashtray. "Now . . . I wanted all of you to hear exactly what will take place between the Russian Premier and myself."

"Mister President," Senator Dee said, "is your position unalterable?"

"Yes, it is."

"Then I think it is a mistake, sir. I am convinced we would win and the Russians would no longer be a threat."

"*You* may be convinced, Senator. And, to tell the truth, I'm convinced that is probably true," the President answered, speaking with deliberate slowness. "But I don't think the tens of millions who would die on both sides would *ever* be convinced it was worth it—that is, of course, if it were possible to have any sort of discussion with the dead. No, Senator, I don't think you, or anyone, would be able to convince them that their death was worth something."

"Then you do mean to tell the Russians," Koss said.

The President nodded.

Koss pursed his lips. "I cannot support you," he said after a few moments.

The President looked at Dee.

"No," Dee said. "I'm sorry, sir, but I'm afraid not."

"Well," Andrews said, "I asked for your opinions, not your support, though God knows I'd like it. The decision is mine and I'll take the responsibility." He reached to his right and picked up the red phone waiting for him on the table.

The phone was part of the Molink System, an elaborate system of teletypes and translators that gave each of the participants the illusion he was in direct voice contact with his counterpart. Neither the President nor the Premier ever heard the voice of the other. Andrews didn't like the deception. The Premier spoke English fluently, yet the insanity of national pride had to rule, rather than reason. If he were able to speak Russian, Andrews thought, he'd *speak* to the Premier in Russian and the hell with national pride.

"Mister Premier," the President said, "I am not going to waste time with small talk. I have something very important to tell you."

"I am listening, Mister President," the Premier answered.

"In approximately two hours, an American missile-carrying submarine will enter the Aegean Sea. It intends to launch its missiles against Russian cities."

There was a pause.

Then: "Why are you telling me this, Mister President? Do you expect me to bargain with you?"

"Mister Premier, the submarine I speak of is the *Barracuda*. Does that name mean anything to you?"

There was another pause, longer this time. Andrews guessed the Premier had asked a member of his staff the question.

"That was the name of your submarine that sank off Chile," the Premier said, coming back on.

"Mister Premier, it did not sink. We have just found out, only hours ago, that the officers aboard are extremists. They wish to involve our two nations in a war." Andrews was perspiring heavily now. He had great difficulty not giving way to the desire to shout. "These men have taken *control* of the *Barracuda,* Mister Premier, and we are certain they intend to launch missiles aboard the submarine against your cities."

"Does that explain the sudden increase in military activity in the Mediterranean?"

"Yes, we have been trying to find the *Barracuda* and destroy her."

"Excuse me, Mister President, but I find it hard to believe that you would destroy one of your own submarines," the Premier said.

"I'd rather destroy one of our *submarines* than many of our *cities,*" Andrews replied.

"I am told you have ground troops moving close to the German-Polish frontier."

The President put his hand over the mouthpiece. "What the *hell* does he mean we have ground troops moving up to the German-Polish frontier?"

"There's a NATO exercise in progress," Admiral Darlin said.

"Then why the hell didn't you signal them to call it *off?*" He uncupped the phone. "Mister Premier? I've just been told it's part of NATO exercises. It has no connection whatever to the presence of the *Barracuda* in water close to your country. Mister Premier, I have called you because in the past we have been able to come to a reasonable solution of our mutual problems. I do not want a war. I know you do not want a war."

"That is true."

"We plan to continue our massive sea and air hunt. But to increase our chances, Admiral Darlin, my Navy Chief of Staff, is here and ready to give his counterpart on your side the necessary technical information. Perhaps you will be able to find the *Barracuda* before she releases her missiles."

"Mister President," the Premier said quietly, "if we have incoming missiles, we will have no choice but to launch our own missiles against your cities. It will be unreasonable, I grant you. But at that point, reasonableness will no longer be an instrument of diplomacy."

"I under*stand* that, Mister Premier, but please . . . we have little time. Darlin will give you all the technical data relating to the *Barracuda,* if you find her—"

"We will not hesitate to destroy her."

President Andrews handed the phone to Darlin. "Tell them everything," he said. "And I mean everything." Then he picked up his cigar and tried to light it. The conversation had gone as he had expected—but not as he hoped it would.

After a few minutes, Darlin returned the phone to the President. "The Premier would like to speak with you again."

"Yes, Mister Premier?"

"I hope war will not become a reality," the Premier said. "I would find it hard to consider you, Mister President, an enemy."

"Thank you, Mister Premier," Andrews answered. "I wish you good luck."

There was nothing more to say. The President put the red phone down. "Gentlemen," he said, his eyes turned down

236

toward the table, "as of this moment the armed forces of this country are on red alert. Admiral Darlin, I want those Russian submarines off our coasts under constant surveillance. They must be sunk if the *Barracuda* is successful."

"Yes, Mister President," Darlin answered.

The President raised his eyes and nodded. Then in a quiet voice he said, "Thank you, gentlemen, thank you. This meeting is at an end. Thank you."

Several hours later, President Andrews, Secretary of State Blakely and all the Joint Chiefs of Staff were in the War Room. They had been there ever since the end of the talk with the Russian Premier. The United States was on a full alert. Every one of the nation's SAC planes was airborne, ready to strike deep into the Russian heartland; the complete arsenal of nuclear missiles had been readied and held at T-90 seconds. All through Europe, American and NATO troops were being deployed to defend the eastern borders of the western European countries.

The monotone voices of the men who manned the huge display system created a constant hum that contrasted sharply with the constant chatter of the printout machines. The entire armed might of the United States was being moved to protect the country from a Russian retaliatory strike.

A communications system had been set up to allow the President to speak directly to any pilot, ship captain or field officer needed. Another device allowed the President and all members of his staff to hear all Russian communications in instantaneous translation.

There was no conversation between the President and the men around him. He had watched the board for hours without speaking, and when anyone near him spoke, he silenced them with a wave of his hand, or a look.

Though the temperature in the room was always held at precisely sixty-five degrees and the humidity at twenty percent, the President was sweating profusely. Each time a plane in the Mediterranean reported back to its base, or one pilot spoke to another, he moved forward and checked the position of the aircraft on the display board.

Never had he felt so tired, not even during the exhausting days at the end of the campaign, when he had gone to ten cities in one day and made as many speeches. That kind of fatigue had had a different feel to it, a kind of exhilaration, in comparison to the total deadening physical and mental exhaustion that came over him now. He wondered if the Premier was feeling the same way.

"Mister President," Blakely told him, "word has come that Captain Richard's son is safe."

He looked at his Secretary of State and nodded. "Thank God for that at least. Now let's hope he'll have something to be safe for." And he turned his attention back to the board.

Suddenly an American pilot said, "This is Bluejay 6 . . . Bluejay 6 to Mother 4 . . . Bluejay 6 to Mother 4."

"Mother 4. Go ahead, Bluejay 6."

"Positive reading," the pilot said, giving the coordinates. "Do you read me? *Positive* reading."

"Five by five, Bluejay 6. Can you hold it?"

"Will try."

The President was on his feet. In front of him, the screen quickly showed the position of Bluejay 6 and his carrier, Mother 4. The plane was over the eastern Mediterranean, just a hundred miles from the entrance to the Aegean.

Mother 4 was off the south coast of Crete.

"Bluejay 6 . . . Bluejay 6," a radio operator said. "Can you ID the goblin?"

"Negative, Mother 4. Negative."

Suddenly, the President picked up the special mike and pressed the button. "Bluejay 6, this is the President . . . We need a positive ID."

"Who the hell is that joker?" the pilot asked. "I've got enough problems without—"

"It's *no joker,*" the President said.

"Bluejay 6, this is Mother 4. You are in direct communication with the President."

There was no answer from Bluejay 6.

"Listen," Andrews said, "can you give us a positive ID, Bluejay 6?"

"No, sir."

"Why the hell not?" Andrews almost shouted.

"Sir, trouble . . . Two bandits at three o'clock."

Suddenly, the second communication system came on. "I see the plane," one of the Russian pilots said. "Signal him off. If he refuses to turn, shoot him down."

"Bluejay 6," Andrews said, "get out of there. Get out of there!"

"I read you," the pilot answered. "Mother 4, making a one hundred and eighty degree turn."

"Contact with submarine," a Russian pilot said. "Contact . . . killer pack two . . . submarine my position."

"Killer pack two moving in," another voice announced.

The President turned to Admiral Darlin. "What the hell is going on?"

"They found the *Barracuda,*" the Admiral answered.

"Launching anti-sub missiles," the Russian pilot said.

"Missiles launched . . . We have contact!" Then something like a sigh. "It is over."

The President put the mike down. "It is over," he repeated quietly. "It is over. Tomorrow we will begin the work of finding out how it all started . . ." He shook his head and, wiping his brow, said, "Cancel the alert . . . it is over." He turned and walked slowly to the door of the War Room, hoping his knees would not buckle under him. . . .

"Ladies and gentlemen," the television newscaster said, "tonight hundreds of American planes and ships are moving toward the Mediterranean Sea in what is an almost unprecedented military movement. The White House, the Pentagon, the State Department, the Defense Department —nobody is speaking, but there is no doubt that we are in the midst of an unspecified crisis of major proportions. Reports from the Middle East are tangled and confused. One unconfirmed report tells of hard fighting between Israeli and Syrian troops on the Golan Heights. Another tells of clashes between planes from our Sixth Fleet and Russian fighters who, it is claimed, are attempting to strafe and bomb the Israeli positions on the Golan Heights. Again, *none* of this is confirmed. The only thing that is certain is that American ships and planes *are* on the move, and no one in the government is talking. From Washington here is a report from our correspondent—"

Richard leaned forward and switched off the TV.

"Don't you want to see the rest of the news?" Hilary asked. She was sitting beside him on the sofa in her apartment, where they had gone after eating at the Sea Catch.

He shook his head.

"Nathan . . . that's why you've been so edgy all night,

hasn't it? I mean, the crisis—you knew about it, didn't you? That's what's kept you so frantic all day."

He stood up. "Maybe tonight was the wrong—"

Hilary was on her feet. She came against him. "Don't say it. Don't say it." And before he could speak, she kissed him on the lips, long and hard. His arms went about her and he returned her kiss. "It *has* been a difficult time," he said. "And maybe it will become even more difficult."

"Because of what they said on the news? Nathan, what *is* happening? Can you talk about it?"

"No. It's better not to talk about it," he said, nuzzling her hair. "Hilary, right this moment, all that really matters is that I'm with you."

"Do you really mean that?"

"I'll show you," he answered and, quickly reaching down, picked her up and carried her into the bedroom. "When I could," he told her, "I thought about you today." He set her down and slowly opened the buttons of her blouse.

"A more ardent lover would have said he thought about me *all* day."

"Really." He reached around to undo her bra and bent down to kiss each breast as soon as it was bare.

She put her arms around his neck. "I thought about you today, too," she told him.

"It sounds wonderful," he said.

She reached down and unbuckled his belt.

In moments they were naked together, joined in desire, their bodies moving to the rhythm of their need. Hilary clutched at Richard, between her thighs, moaning with delight.

"I love you," she cried out at the height of her passion. "Oh God, I do love you!"

And holding her tight, tighter than he had held anyone in years, he answered, "Me too . . . Marry me, Hilary . . . Marry me!"

"Yes, my darling, yes . . ."

Out of breath and full of the afterglow of their lovemaking, they lay wrapped in each other's arms.

"I meant it," Richard said. "I really do want to marry you."

She moved her hand through his hair. "I meant it too," she told him.

"I don't want to wait," he said, thinking of how lonely he had been the last few years, all the women who had come and gone in the night and left him feeling empty.

"Neither do I."

He sat up. "It won't be easy. I've made some enemies—"

"I don't want to talk about that now," she replied, gently pulling him down beside her again. "I only want to be close to you." And to give emphasis to her words, she clasped his thigh between hers.

Richard held her breast and with his face close to hers, fell asleep, thinking of the years to—the ringing of the telephone slashed into his brain. He opened his eyes and blinked.

"It's for you," Hilary said, yawning and fumbling the phone to him.

Richard cleared his throat and shook his head. "Captain Richard."

"This is Goree."

"Yes, Captain." Richard was suddenly awake. "What's happened?"

"Sorry to wake you up, but I promised to call if there was any news. We got it."

"We—?"

"I should say they. We think it was one of their killer subs. Naturally, they won't give us any details about how they managed it."

Richard sighed. "Thank you. Thank you *very* much, Captain Goree. And thank Admiral Powell for me . . . I'm glad it's over."

"One part of it, anyway," Goree answered. "Now come the repercussions. One hundred and forty American men dead aboard the *Barracuda,* the Russians receiving secret information, the Russians destroying one of our subs . . . You did your duty, Captain—but not everyone will see it that way. I hope you're *ready* for it, Captain."

Before Richard could answer, the line went dead.

"Is anything wrong?" Hilary asked.

Richard handed the phone back to her. "No . . . no . . . it's all right." Goree's words made him shake his head, the sound of his voice . . . it was almost as if Goree himself were accusing him. He remembered Goree's warning about Crawton's powerful friends, "I hope you're ready for it, Captain."

Suddenly, a chill ran down Richard's back. Goree? Could *Goree* be one of them? Someone had fed inside information to the conspirators all day. Someone had called Fioredeliso from the Pentagon and told him where Henry was. Only a handful of men had even *known* Henry was missing. Could it have been—

"Nathan? Nathan, darling, what did you say?"

Richard hadn't realized he'd been talking aloud. "Nothing, Hilary, go back to sleep . . . I know this all sounds strange but in a few days it will all be in the newspapers and then maybe you'll understand." He took her in his arms. "I just think you should know that phone call . . . makes me a poor risk . . . as husband, or anything else."

"You're not trying to back off?"

"No. I just wanted you to know . . . what I said before. Things—"

She put a finger to his lips. "Trust me," she said, hugging him tightly to her bare breasts. "Trust me. As long as we're together and I can watch over you, you'll be fine."

Richard put his lips to hers and kissed her for a long, long time. Afterwards, he whispered, "Tomorrow—would you like to meet my son, and my folks?"

"Yes, I would love to. I would like to meet everyone who is important to you, everyone. . . ."

Saturday, November 18th. Ship time: 1400. We are on the bottom. We are dying. At 0600, two hundred nautical miles from our target area we were mortally wounded by three antisubmarine missiles. There is no way of knowing whether they came from our own ships or planes, or from Russian. The first missile struck the missile compartment, killing everyone in it. The second blew away most of our sail and the hydrothermal sensing devices on it. The third damaged part of our engine room. It makes no difference. Our sensing devices were damaged anyway. Sabotage. It was what I was afraid of. One of the dissidents on board sabotaged the mechanisms. We were sitting ducks.

We are almost four hundred meters down, far too deep to launch our missiles. We are—that is, those of us who are left—all dead men. Sooner or later, either the Russians or our own forces will make further contact with us and then—

I did not think our glorious mission could possibly end this way. It will be very slow. The air will die and then the rest of us will die.

I am frightened, so very frightened.

The ventilation system is out and the lights are very dim. We are taking on water and the smell of oil is everywhere.

I have chosen to stay in my quarters. The men are dispersed through what is left of the boat. Some are crying, others are praying. I can do neither.

They have found us. The attack has begun.

End and final entry of Captain Crawton, Commander of the submarine *Barracuda*. . . .